BIG SOFTIES

BIG SOFTIES

35 great designer knits in mohair

Melinda Coss

AURUM PRESS

For my colleagues and friends, the knitting editors, with thanks
for their hard work and unfailing encouragement.

First published 1992 by Aurum Press Limited,
10 Museum Street, London WC1A 1JS
Copyright © Melinda Coss 1992

A catalogue record for this book is available from the British Library.

ISBN 1 85410 222 2

1 3 5 7 9 10 8 6 4 2
1993 1995 1996 1994 1992

Typeset by Dorchester Typesetting Group Ltd
Printed and bound in Italy by New Interlitho SpA, Milan

CONTENTS

ABBREVIATIONS 6
ACKNOWLEDGEMENTS 6
INTRODUCTION 7
TECHNIQUES 8

ALL SQUARE JUMPER 10
COAT OF MANY COLOURS 12
MUSTANG JUMPER 17
SQUARE DANCE JUMPER 18
FOUR-NIGHT KNIT JUMPER 21
ANEMONE JACKET 22
SLIPSTITCH JUMPER 24
SHELL JACKET AND COAT 25
FLASH ARROWS JUMPER 28
DOGTOOTH COAT 30
HARLEQUIN COAT 32
'EXCLUSIVELY YOURS' COAT 34
MAN'S GEOMETRIC SWEATER 36
RAZZLE DAZZLE JACKET AND COAT 38
FANTASY JUMPER 41
WARM ROSE JACKET 45
PATCHWORK JACKET 48
ARGYLL COAT 50
PRISCILLA COAT 53
PIERROT JUMPER 59
ARIZONA JACKET 61
FLOWER GARDEN JACKET 63
CUT-A-DASH JACKET 68
FLAGSHIP JACKET 70
SOFT OPTION JACKET 72
REFLECTIONS JACKET 74
SPLASH OF PINK COAT 76
ZIGZAG AND BOBBLES JACKET 80
DIAMOND JACKET 82
STRIKE UP THE BAND JACKET 84
'SOFTLY SPEAKING' JACKET 86
INCA JACKET 88
CLASSIC CREW-NECKED CARDIGAN AND SWEATER 90
JIGSAW JACKET 92
RING-A-ROUND COAT 94

STOCKIST INFORMATION 96

ABBREVIATIONS

alt	alternate(ly)
beg	begin(ning)
cm	centimetre(s)
cont	continue(ing)
dec	decrease(ing)
foll	follow(ing)
in	inch(es)
inc	increase(ing)
k	knit
MB	make bobble
m1	make 1 stitch (i.e. work into the stitch below the next stitch to be worked)
p	purl
psso	pass slip stitch over
rem	remaining
rep	repeat
RS(s)	right side(s)
sl	slip
st(s)	stitch(es)
st st	stocking stitch
tog	together
WS(s)	wrong side(s)
yfwd	yarn forward
yon	yarn over needle
yrn	yarn round needle

ACKNOWLEDGEMENTS

Thanks are due to the following for permission to reproduce published patterns: Shirley Bradford (*Woman*), Theresa Cawthorne (*Bella*), Mary Eddy (*Woman and Home*), Peggy Greedus (*Woman's Realm*), Marion Smith (*Woman's Weekly*); H. Bauer Publishing, IPC Publishers, Marshall Cavendish Partworks Ltd. And to the following photographers for permission to reproduce photographs: Nigel Limb (Razzle Dazzle jacket and coat, p.39), Peter Waldman (Ring-a-Round coat, p.94, and Flash Arrows jumper, p.29). Grateful thanks also to Peter Smith of Scaioni's Studio for his photography (pp. 2, 45, 46, 47, 73, 75, 90, 91, 93). And to Kate Simunek for permission to reproduce the line illustrations on pp. 8 and 9.

The patterns listed below were first published in the magazines to which they are attributed:
Bella: Flash Arrows jumper, Harlequin coat, Razzle Dazzle jacket and coat, Ring-a-Round coat.
Daily Express: Four-Night Knit jumper.
Get Knitting (Marshall Cavendish): Anemone jacket, Fantasy jumper, Man's geometric sweater, Mustang jumper.
Sunday Mirror: Square Dance jumper.
Woman: Shell jacket and coat, Reflections jacket, Diamond jacket.
Woman and Home: Coat of Many Colours, Splash of Pink coat, Strike up the Band jacket, Warm Rose jacket.
Woman's Realm: All Square jumper, Argyll coat, Dogtooth coat, 'Exclusively Yours' coat, Patchwork jacket.
Woman's Weekly: Soft Option jacket, 'Softly Speaking' jacket.

INTRODUCTION

My very first attempt at knitting produced a big, baggy, V-necked, lilac-coloured mohair jumper. It was back in the early Sixties and I wore it with black stockings, dangly earrings, backcombed hair, false eyelashes, white lipstick and a big silver medallion. Thirty years on, here we are again in our long mohair jumpers with tight black leggings. The hair and make-up are different, but the look is timeless.

Mohair is the perfect knitting yarn. It is great for beginners because the fluffiness conceals mistakes. It is knitted on big needles, so making a jumper is not a lifetime's work, and the fluffy texture has enough impact to eliminate the need for fancy stitches and complicated shapes. Mohair is light to wear, warm in winter, and perfect for spring/summer cardigans and jackets. It can look pretty and feminine or bold and sporty and, provided you do not throw them in the washing machine, your knits will last for ever.

I have been designing knitwear for eight years now. Two years into my career, Peggy Greedus of *Woman's Realm* approached me to produce a design specially for her magazine. It seemed sensible to offer her readers the choice of either buying their own mohair from a wool shop or ordering a kit for the design directly from me. The response to that first kit offer was staggering and, over the years, I have had the pleasure of working with most of the knitting editors of the major women's magazines and of serving their readers in the same way. We now have over 10,000 knitting-kit customers on our mailing list and, while I often produce designs in wool and cotton, the response to the mohair designs is at least ten times greater than the response to those using other yarns.

The following designs are firm favourites with my customers. Many of the designs have appeared in magazines and are reproduced with the kind permission of their editors. Some are several years old, but none has dated. I hope you enjoy making them as much as I enjoyed designing them.

Melinda Coss.

TECHNIQUES

TENSION

Tension is by far the most important and most abused rule in knitting. The word is used quite simply to describe the number of rows and stitches you will achieve for every 10cm (4in) you knit. This is determined not only by the size of needle you use, but also by the thickness of yarn, the stitch pattern and sometimes even by the colour of the yarn, since some dyes will leave yarns fluffy and others will give a dense effect. When a pattern is written, it is calculated mathematically and, providing your tension is as stated on the pattern, the garment will knit up to the actual size that is quoted. The method you have used will also influence the tension. For example, it is a common mistake to pull yarns too tightly across the back of the work when knitting using the fairisle method. This can reduce the size of a garment by as much as 15cm (6in) in width. The phone calls I always dread are from 'expert' knitters who call to complain that their garment has not knitted up to size. 'Did you do a tension swatch?' I ask. 'No, but I've been knitting for years' is the common reply.

A tension swatch should be knitted before beginning any piece of work. Cast on the number of stitches quoted in your pattern as equal to 10cm (4in), and then add on four extra. Knit or pattern the number of rows stated in the row tension and cast off. Lay the sample of knitting on a flat surface and, using a ruler, count the number of stitches and rows *you* get to 10cm (4in). If you get fewer than

Use a ruler and pins to measure the tension of a sample piece of knitting.

recommended, use needles that are half a size smaller. If you get more, use needles that are half a size bigger. It takes around 20 minutes to check your tension. If you don't bother, you risk spending days making up a jumper that turns out to be the wrong size.

For some knitters it is simply impossible to achieve the right number of rows and stitches. When this is the case, get as close as you can to the stitch tension rather than the row tension, and add or deduct a few rows on the welts or at the top of the garment to meet the correct length. Tensions given are for average knitters but, in reality, there is no such thing, so do yourself a favour and check your personal tension before you begin.

CHARTS

Many people suffer from a fear of charts, but I promise you they really are easy. All you need to remember is that every little square represents a

stitch, and every row of squares represents a row of knitting. Your cast-on row is *not* shown on the chart, so the first row of squares is (unless stated otherwise in the text) a knit row. With knit rows you read the chart from right to left. Once the first row is worked you move up a row and, working in purl, read the chart from left to right. If the garment is shaped, then decreases or increases are clearly shown at the appropriate edges of the charts and are drawn *at the bottom* of the row on which they occur.

It is helpful to take a photostat of your chart and mark each row off as you complete it. Note also that the charts are divided into blocks of ten stitches and ten rows, which makes it easy to count large single-coloured areas. Go on, have a go. You will miss out on making up some lovely designs if you do not master the technique.

SIZING

Most of my designs are produced in one size only and the majority are worked on 5½mm (no. 5) needles. If you want to make the garment smaller, reduce your needle size by half; to make it bigger, increase by half. It is not wise to go to smaller than a 5mm (no. 6) needle, since the fabric will become too dense, but you can go up to a 7mm (no. 2) needle for larger sizes. Remember that the more loosely you knit, the more yarn you use, and take this into account when buying your mohair. Many of the designs have dropped sleeves, so it is easy to adjust the sleeve length by leaving a bit off the top or making the welts shorter. I have always assumed that people who like mohair jumpers generally appreciate them being big and baggy. You will find my shapes easy to wear, and the coats leave lots of room for winter undergarments.

INTARSIA

This is simply a fancy word for a method of multicolour knitting where you *do not* carry the yarn that is not in use across the back of the work, but use separate balls of each colour and join them in as you need them. The biggest problem with intarsia is that the numerous little balls dangling at the back tend to get into a terrible muddle. When you are using mohair

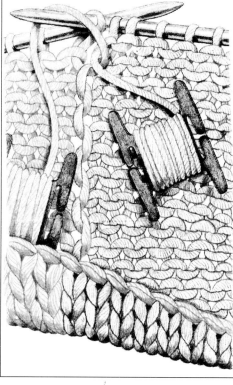

If you are using the intarsia method, twist the yarns firmly together when you change colours.

they can be a real headache to untangle. To minimize this situation it is a good idea to wind each individual colour that you are using around a cardboard or plastic bobbin. This adds extra weight to the yarn, and the separate balls can then easily be unmuddled at the end of a row. Make sure that loose ends are left long enough to be threaded and secured at the back of the work with a tapestry needle.

When changing colours in the middle of a row, the most important thing to remember is to cross the two colours at the back of the work to avoid making a hole. If you have never knitted with lots of colours before, start with something simple like 'All Square' (see p. 10). Once you have mastered two or three colours you will have the skill to attack a design like 'Fantasy' (p. 37) or 'Priscilla' (p. 45). All the designs in this book are primarily stocking stitch and very simple to knit, and the only reason that some appear complicated is because of the number of colours used. However, once you can use three colours in one design, you can just as easily use twenty – it is exactly the same technique.

FAIRISLE

Fairisle knitting is a technique, although many people confuse the term with the glorious designs from the Fair Isles, which are traditional patterns that this technique is used to achieve. Using the fairisle method, when two colours are in work, you carry the colour not in use across the back of your knitting, catching it every few stitches. Some knitters are used to catching in the yarn at the back of every stitch (i.e. 'weaving in'), but this is not recommended when working with mohair, since it produces too dense a fabric. The most important thing to remember is not to pull your yarn too tightly across the back, since this will distort the size and shape of the garment. While I strongly recommend knitting a tension swatch before beginning any piece of work, it is particularly advisable when working using the fairisle method, since this is where most of the sizing mistakes occur. Also, please do *not* use this method when told to work in intarsia as you will not be happy with the result and you may well find yourself short of yarn.

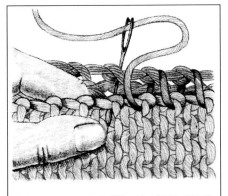

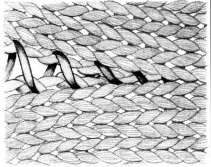

The diagrams show how you should hold the knitting to work a flat seam and how the work will look on the right side.

MAKING UP

Lumpy seams can ruin a beautifully knitted garment, so try to use flat seams where possible and be especially careful where collars join at the back of the neck and on cuff seams, which are visible when turned back. Main seams can be sewn in narrow backstitch, and it is always advisable to pin the seams first to make sure they match. Be careful also to match the colours and stripes where appropriate. Invisible seams can be achieved by oversewing at the very edge, that is, by lining up the two pieces of work you are joining and sewing through the two stitches that lie directly opposite each other at the very edge of your work. This will give you a completely flat effect and you should not even be able to see where you have joined the two pieces.

THE MOST COMMON QUESTIONS AND THEIR ANSWERS

What is a 'Mo'

I am afraid there is no such animal as a 'mo'. The name 'mohair' comes from the Arabic *Mukhayyar*, meaning 'choice' or 'select'. This is a highly appropriate name for a wonderful yarn which is light, hard-wearing, lustrous and warm. Mohair comes from the Angora goat, which in turn was named after the region in Turkey. Nowadays, however, mohair goats are bred worldwide, and I even have some living next door to me in Wales. They are lovely creatures with angelic, smiling faces and long, curly coats. Their temperament is more sheeplike than goatlike, and I would strongly recommend them as pets if you feel like going into competition with me.

How do I prevent the yarn from shedding?

This is difficult because with any long-haired yarn, and especially a natural yarn, fibres are bound to fly. Some people suggest placing your wool in the fridge before working with it, but the only result I have got from that is chilblains from working with icy-cold yarn. The most reliable remedy is to wear a cover-up while you are working and to get the garment dry-cleaned once after you have completed it. This will get rid of a lot of loose fibres.

Does mohair itch?

Some people are extremely sensitive to natural fibres, of which mohair is one. However, I like to think that our mohair is softer and silkier than most and, since it is a mix of 83 per cent mohair, 9 per cent wool and 8 per cent nylon, it is also hard-wearing and practical. It is not a yarn that should be worn by asthmatics or babies, but then neither is pure wool. The main reason I produce more jacket designs than jumpers is that I feel natural fibres are best worn away from the skin, when they can be sported in absolute comfort.

How do I care for my completed garment?

Mohair should be hand-washed in cool water and a speciality soap liquid. We are currently offering a new formula called 'Purity' to our customers, which is a wonderful naturally based washing-liquid formulated especially for use with mohair. Alternatively, you should use Woolite or Stergene for the best results. Dry the garment flat, laying it over a clotheshorse so that the air can circulate, and brush it up with a hairbrush when it is completely dry. Another tip, if you own a tumble dryer, is to wait until the garment is completely dry and then put it in your machine for no more than three or four rotations of the drum – just long enough to create static but not long enough to subject the garment to intense heat. The static effect makes the fibres stand on end in restored fluffiness. Always store your mohair garments flat . . . if you hang them up they will grow!

ALL SQUARE JUMPER

This was the very first kit that I produced. It is strange how fashions revolve. Block designs are filling the magazines again this season, and this one is simple to knit and snug to wear for any fun occasion. Work using the intarsia method (see p. 8).

(see p. 8).

SIZE To fit bust 86–96/96–107cm (34–38/38–42in). Actual sizes: 104–117cm (41–46in) bust; 69.5/75.5cm (27^1/$_4$/29^3/$_4$in) long; 50/54.5cm (19^1/$_2$/21^1/$_2$in) sleeve.

MATERIALS Melinda Coss Mohair: Red (A) 225gm, Emerald (B) 125gm, Turquoise (C) 100gm, Yellow (D) 115gm, Black (E) 100gm.

NEEDLES One pair of 4/4^1/$_2$mm (no. 8/7) needles and one pair of 5/6mm (no. 6/4) needles. Spare needles.

TENSION Using 5mm (no. 6) needles and measured over st st, 18 sts and 20 rows = 10cm square (4in square); using 6mm (no. 4) needles and measured over st st, 16 sts and 19 rows = 10cm square (4in square).

NB Instructions for the two sizes are given as smaller/larger; when only one figure is given, it applies to both sizes.

BACK

Using 4/4^1/$_2$mm (no. 8/7) needles and A, cast on 84 sts. Work in k1, pl rib for 16 rows.
Next row: rib 1, *inc in next st, rib 9*, rep from * to * 8 times, inc in next st, rib to end (94 sts).
Change to 5/6mm (no. 6/4) needles and work in pattern as follows.
Row 1 (RS): k21A, k2E, k23B, k2E, k23C, k2E, k21D.
Row 2: p21D, k2E, p23C, k2E, p23B, k2E, p21A.
Rows 3–24: work in pattern as set.
Rows 25 and 26: knit in E.
Rows 27–52: work as rows 1–26 but reading D for A, C for B, A for C and B for D.
Rows 53–78: work as rows 1–26 but reading C for A, D for C and C for D.
Rows 79–104: work as rows 1–26 but reading D for B and B for D.
Rows 105–130: work as rows 1–26 but reading D for A, D for C and A for D. Cast off.

FRONT

Work as for back until row 80 of pattern has been worked, then **divide for neck.**

Row 81: k21A, k2E, k6D, turn and leave rem sts on a spare needle.
Work on first set of sts as follows.
Work straight in pattern as set until row 104 of pattern has been completed.
Row 105: k21D, k2E, k6B.
Row 106: p6B, k2E, p21D.
Work 22 rows in pattern as set.
Rows 129 and 130: work as rows 25 and 26. Cast off.
Return to sts held on spare needle and, with RS facing, join in yarn to inner end. Cast off 36 sts and work pattern to end. Work straight in pattern as set until row 104 of pattern has been completed.
Row 105: k6D, k2E, k21A.
Row 106: p21A, k2E, p6D.
Work 22 rows in pattern as set.
Rows 129 and 130: work as rows 25 and 26. Cast off.

SLEEVES

(Both alike.) Using 4/4^1/$_2$mm (no. 8/7) needles and A, cast on 38 sts. Work in k1, p1 rib for 16 rows.
Next row: rib 2, (inc in next st, rib 1), rep to end.
Change to 5/6mm (no. 6/4) needles.
Row 1 (RS): k3C, k2E, k22B, k2E, k22A, k2E, k3C.
Row 2: p3C, k2E, p22A, k2E, p22B, k2E, p3C.
Rows 3–10: rep rows 1 and 2 four times, inc 1 st at each end of rows 3 and 9.
Rows 11 and 12: knit in E.
Row 13: k5A, k2E, k22C, k2E, k22D, k2E, k5A.
Row 14: p5A, k2E, p22D, k2E, p22C, p2E, p5A.
Inc 1 st each end of next and every foll sixth row until there are 84 sts (taking extra sts in pattern as necessary), work in pattern as follows.
Work 22 rows in pattern as set.
Rows 37 and 38: work as rows 11 and 12.
Row 39: using C, inc in first st, k8C, k2E, k22A, k2E, k22B, k2E, k8C, using C, inc in last st.
Row 40: p10C, k2E, p22B, k2E, p22A, k2E, p10C.
Work 22 rows in pattern as set.
Row 63: using E, inc in first st, knit to last st, inc in last st.
Row 64: knit in E.
Row 65: k14D, k2E, k22B, k2E, k22C, k2E, k14D.
Row 66: p14D, k2E, p22C, k2E, p22B, k2E, p14D.
Work 14 rows in pattern as set.
Row 81: using D, inc in first st, k15D, k2E, k22B, k2E, k22C, k15D, using D, inc in last st (84 sts).
Work straight for 7 rows.
Rows 89 and 90: work as rows 11 and 12. Cast off loosely.

COLLAR

Using 4/4½mm (no. 8/7) needles and A, cast on 138 sts. Work in k1, p1 rib for 20.5cm (8in). Cast off loosely in rib.

MAKING UP

Join shoulder seams. Sew sleeves in place, matching centre of each sleeve top to shoulder seam, then join side and sleeve seams. Sew cast-on edge of collar to neck, overlapping row ends and sewing them to cast-off sts at base of neck opening.

COAT OF MANY COLOURS

'Entrelac', from the French *entrelacer*, means to interlace or intertwine. The finished work, which is made of zigzag panels, gives a woven patchwork effect, although the fabric is knitted in one piece. Entrelac knitting is easier than it looks and has the advantage of enabling you to use up all those odd bits of yarn. This three-quarter-length coat with its rich jewel colours is a perfect cover-up for autumn.

SIZE To fit bust 86–92cm (34–36in). Actual size: 125cm (49in) bust; 57cm (22¼in) side seam; 43cm (17in) sleeve with cuff turned back.

MATERIALS Melinda Coss Mohair: Black (main colour, 1) 200gm, Emerald (2) 75gm, Bottle Green (3) 75gm, Fuchsia (4) 75gm, Royal (5) 75gm, Purple (6) 75gm, Navy (7) 75gm, Maroon (8) 75gm, Slate (9) 75gm, Turquoise (10) 75gm. 9 buttons.

NEEDLES One pair of 4½mm (no. 7) needles and one pair of 5mm (no. 6) needles.

TENSION Using 5mm (no. 6) needles and measured over st st pattern, each rectangle = 5cm (2in) across and 6cm (2½in) deep.

BACK

Using 5mm (no. 6) needles and black, cast on 66 sts. Work in garter stitch (knit every row) for 3cm (1¼in), ending with a RS row. Knit 1 more row, dec 1 st at each end. Beg entrelac pattern, changing colour when each individual triangle or rectangle is started. **Form base triangles.**
Row 1 (WS): using first colour, p2, turn.
Row 2: k2, turn.
Row 3: p3 (purling extra st from left-hand needle), turn.
Row 4: k3, turn.
Row 5: p4, turn.
Row 6: k4, turn.
Cont as set, adding an extra st on every purl row until there are 8 sts on the right-hand needle, ending with a purl row. This forms one triangle. Work 7 more in the same way so that all 64 sts are on the right-hand needle. **Work selvedge triangle.**
Row 1: k2, turn.
Row 2: p2, turn.
Row 3: inc into the first st, sl1, k1, psso, turn.
Row 4: p3, turn.
Row 5: k1, inc into next st, sl1, k1, psso, turn.
Row 6: p4, turn.
Row 7: k1, inc into next st, k1, sl1, k1, psso, turn.
Row 8: p5, turn.
Row 9: k1, inc into next st, k2, sl1, k1, psso, turn.

Cont as set, inc into the second st on every knit row until there are 8 sts, ending with a knit row.
Work the first rectangle, which is knitted up from the second side of the first base triangle (see diagram for direction of knitting). With RS facing, knit up 8 sts along this edge, working from top to bottom.
Row 1: p8, turn.
Row 2: k7, sl1, k next st from left-hand needle, psso, turn.
Rep these 2 rows until all the sts from the first side of the second triangle have been incorporated. This completes the first rectangle. Work a rectangle from the 6 following triangles, and then, from the second side of the last triangle, form a **selvedge triangle**. Knit up 8 sts as from the previous triangles.
Row 1: p2tog, p6, turn.
Row 2: k7.
Row 3: p2tog, p5, turn.
Cont as set until 1 st remains. Fasten off.
Work another line of rectangles in the opposite direction, beg, with RS facing, by knitting up 8 sts from bottom to top along the inner edge of the selvedge triangle just worked.
Row 1: p7, p2tog (1 st from triangle, 1 st from rectangle).
Row 2: k8.
Keep rep last 2 rows until all the sts from the rectangle have been incorporated. Work rem rectangles as set, finishing by incorporating the sts from the selvedge triangle at the end.*
Rep from * to * 9 times more. To finish with a straight edge form a row of triangles.
Row 1: k2, turn.
Row 2: p2, turn.
Row 3: inc into first st, sl1, k1, psso, turn.
Row 4: p3, turn.
Row 5: k1, inc into next st, sl1, k1, psso, turn.
Row 6: p4, turn.
Row 7: k1, inc into next st, k1, sl1, k1, psso, turn.
Row 8: p5, turn.
Row 9: k2tog, k2, sl1, psso, turn.
Row 10: p4, turn.
Row 11: k2tog, k1, sl1, k1, psso, turn.
Row 12: p3, turn.
Row 13: k2tog, sl1, k1, psso, turn.
Row 14: p2tog, turn. Sl this st on to the right-hand needle and then, with RS facing, knit up 8 sts along the second side of the first rectangle from top to bottom.
Row 1: p7, p2tog.
Row 2: sl1, k1, psso, k5, sl1, k1 (from next rectangle), psso, turn.
Row 3: p7.
Row 4: sl1, k1, psso, k4, sl1, k1, psso, turn.
Row 5: p6.
Cont as set until row p2 has been worked.

Next row: k1, sl1, k1, psso, k1, turn.
Next row: sl1, p2tog, psso.
Work from the next 6 rectangles in the same manner and finish with another triangle, first knitting up 8 sts from the last rectangle as before.
Row 1: p7, p2tog.
Row 2: sl1, k1, psso, k4, k2tog.
Row 3: p6.
Row 4: sl1, k1, psso, k2, k2tog.
Row 5: p4.
Row 6: sl1, k1, psso, k2tog.
Row 7: p2.
Row 8: k2tog and fasten off.

RIGHT FRONT

Using 5mm (no. 6) needles and black, cast on 42 sts. Work in garter st for 3cm (1¼in), ending with a RS row. Knit another row, dec 1 st each end. Now form 4 base triangles and work as for back until * to * has been worked, then rep 8 times more. Then shape neck. Work a selvedge triangle as at top edge of back, fastening off the final st left on the needle. Now cont to work a normal band of rectangles, finishing with an edge selvedge triangle. Now work another band of rectangles in the opposite direction but omit the final one. Turn the work and finish off with triangles as the top of the back.

LEFT FRONT

Work as for right front until * to * has been worked, then rep 8 times more. Beg another band of rectangles, but instead of working the final rectangle, work the final selvedge triangle as on the top of the back. Now work a band of rectangles in the opposite direction but do not knit up any sts from the first selvedge triangle and cast off the first rectangle sts. Now cont working rectangles normally to end and then work the selvedge triangles as for the top of the back.

SLEEVES

(Both alike.) Using 4½mm (no. 7) needles and black, cast on 48 sts. Work in garter st for 14cm (5½in), ending with a RS row. Knit the next row, inc into every sixth st (56 sts).
Change to 5mm (no. 6) needles and form 7 base triangles. Work from * to * 4 times in all. Finish with a row of triangles as for top of back.

COLLAR

Using 5mm (no. 6) needles and black, cast on 86 sts. Work in garter st for 7cm (2¾in).
Change to 4½mm (no. 7) needles and cont in garter st until collar measures 14cm (5½in). Cast off loosely.

LEFT FRONT BAND

Using 4½mm (no. 7) needles and black and with RS facing, knit up 112 sts evenly along the front edge, working from top to bottom. Work in garter st for 8 rows. Cast off.

RIGHT FRONT BAND

Work as for left front band but knit up from bottom to top. Knit 3 rows then **make buttonholes**.
Next row: k3, cast off 2 sts, (k11, cast off 2 sts) rep to last 3 sts, k3.
Next row: knit, casting on 2 sts above those cast off on previous row.
Knit 3 more rows. Cast off.

MAKING UP

Join shoulder seams with a narrow backstitch. Using 5mm (no. 6) needles and black and with RS facing, knit up 78 sts evenly along the top of the right sleeve (10 sts across each triangle, 1 st between each triangle and 1 st at each end), working from left to right. Knit 1 row. Open out the right armhole and knit up 39 sts either side of the shoulder seam in the same way. Knit 1 row, then knit the sleeve and armhole sts tog. Attach the left sleeve in the same way as the right sleeve. Join side and sleeve seams using a flat seam over the cuffs (remembering which part will be RS when they are turned back) and a very narrow backstitch over the pattern. Use a flat seam to attach the collar to the neck edge by the cast-off edge. Sew on buttons to correspond with the buttonholes.

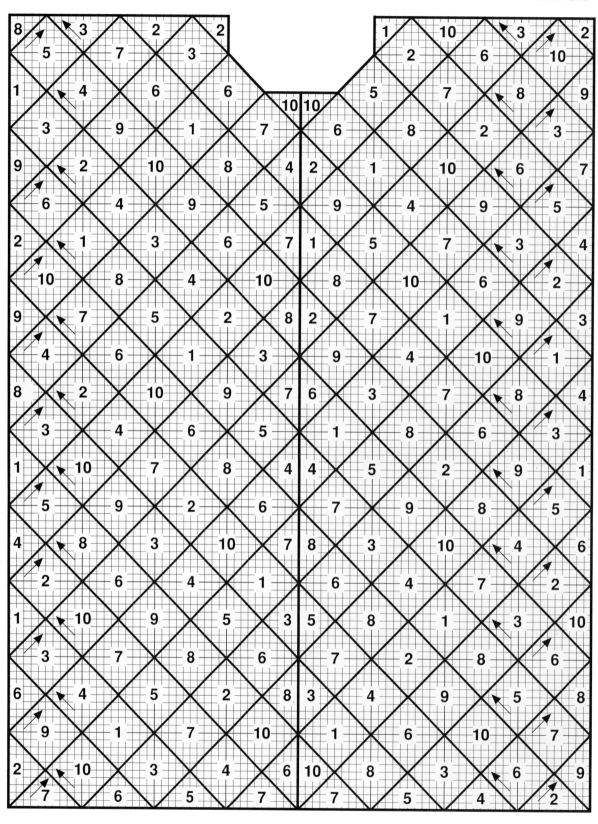

Key   1 = Black   3 = Bottle Green   5 = Royal   7 = Navy   9 = Slate
          2 = Emerald   4 = Fuchsia   6 = Purple   8 = Maroon   10 = Turquoise

Back

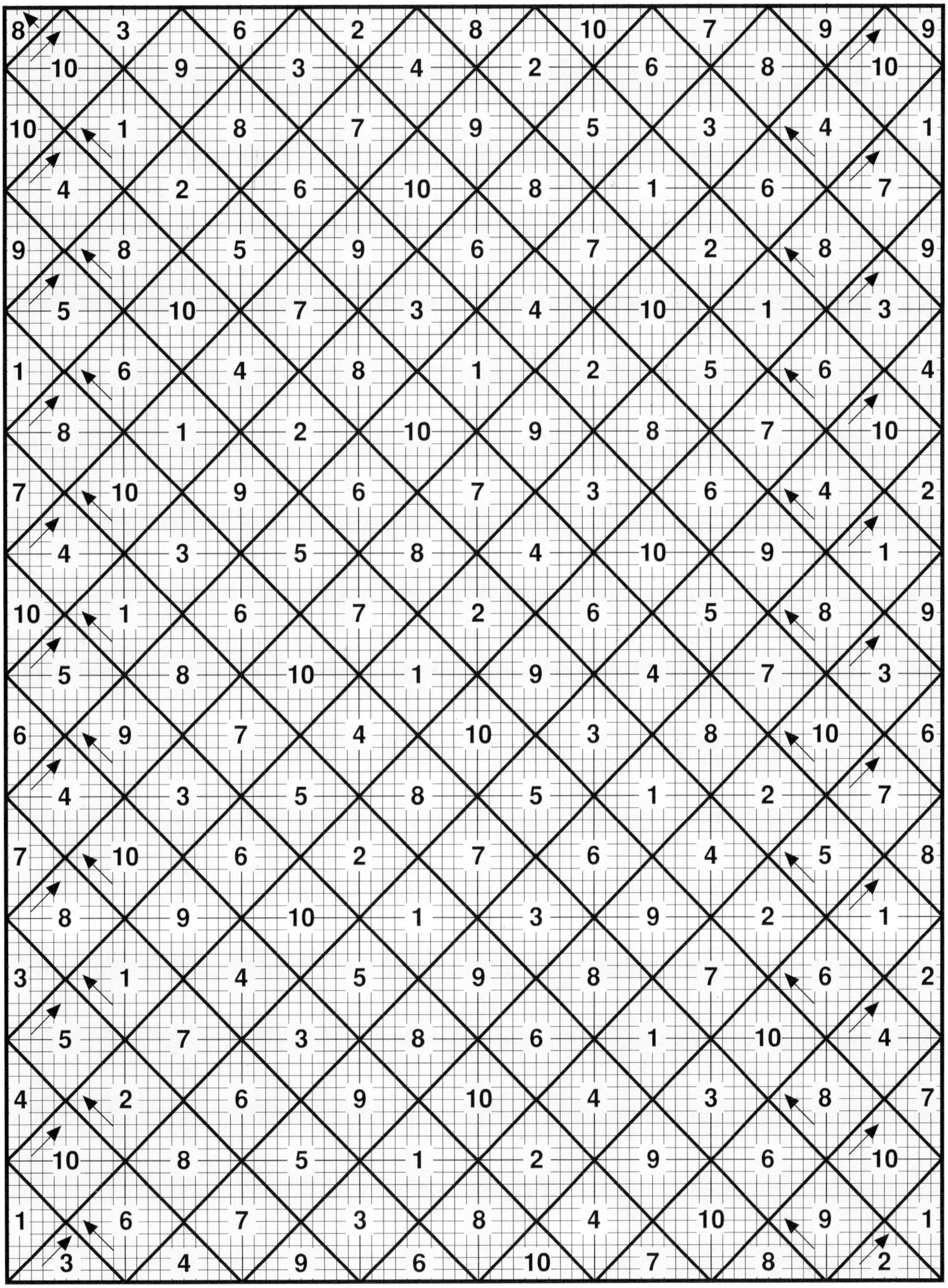

Left Sleeve

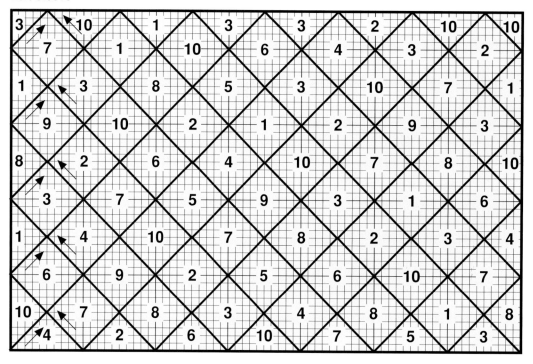

Key

1 = Black	3 = Bottle Green	5 = Royal	7 = Navy	9 = Slate
2 = Emerald	4 = Fuchsia	6 = Purple	8 = Maroon	10 = Turquoise

Right Sleeve

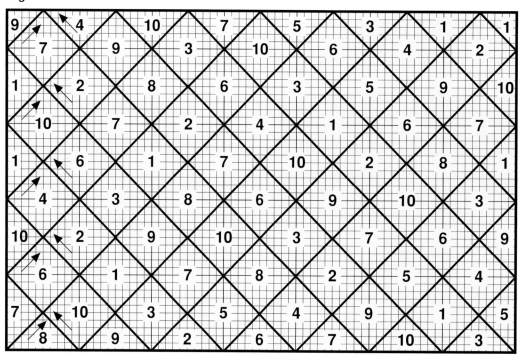

Mustang Jumper

This very simple chunky jumper is knitted with one strand of mohair and one strand of double-knitting cotton. These give a lovely firm fabric when knitted together and add to the appeal of the man for whom, or by whom, this jumper should be knitted!

SIZE To fit chest 100/120cm (39/47in). Actual size: 133/143cm (52½/56½in) chest; 72cm (28½in) long; 36/38cm (14/15in) sleeve.

MATERIALS Melinda Coss Mohair: Yellow 400gm; Melinda Coss DK Cotton: Black 700gm. 3 buttons.

NEEDLES One pair of 7½mm (no. 1) needles.

TENSION Using 7½mm (no. 1) needles and measured over st st, 12 sts and 16 rows = 10cm square (4in square).

NB Use one strand of each yarn together throughout.

BACK

Using 7½mm (no. 1) needles and both yarns, cast on 79/85 sts and work in rib as follows.
Row 1 (RS): k1, (p1, k1) rep to end.
Row 2: p1, (k1, p1) rep to end.
Rep last 2 rows until rib measures 3cm (1¼in), ending with a row 2. Inc 1 st in last row (80/86 sts).
Change to st st and, beg with a knit row, work straight until work measures 40/38cm (15¾/15in). Place a marker at each end of last row and cont straight until work measures 67cm (26¼in), ending with a WS row. **Shape neck.**
Next row: k30/33, turn, leave rem sts on a spare needle.
Next row: cast off 1/2 sts, purl to end.
Next row: knit to end.
Rep last 2 rows until 27 sts rem. Work 1 row. Cast off.
Rejoin yarns to rem sts, cast off centre 20 sts and work to match first side, reversing shapings.

FRONT

Work as for back until work measures 52cm (20½in). **Shape front openings.**
With RS facing, k36/39, turn, leave rem sts on a spare needle.
Cont straight until work measures 67cm (26¼in), ending with a WS row. **Shape neck.**
Next row: k36/39, turn, leave rem sts on a spare needle.
Next row: cast off 3 sts, purl to end.
Next row: knit to end.
Next row: cast off 2/3 sts, purl to end.

Rep last 2 rows until 27 sts rem. Cast off.
Rejoin yarns to rem sts, cast off centre 8 sts and work to match first side, reversing shapings.

SLEEVES

(Both alike.) Using 7½mm (no. 1) needles and both yarns, cast on 29 sts. Work in rib as for back until work measures 3cm (1¼in), inc 2 sts in last row (31 sts).
Change to st st and, beg with a knit row, inc 1 st at each end of this and every foll knit row until there are 77/81 sts. Work straight until work measures 36/38cm (14/15in). Cast off.

COLLAR

Using 7½mm (no. 1) needles and both yarns, cast on 51 sts. Work in rib as for back until work measures 12cm (4¾in). Cast off loosely in rib.

BUTTONHOLE BAND

Using 7½mm (no. 1) needles and both yarns, cast on 8 sts and work in k1, p1 rib for 4cm (1½in).
Next row (make buttonhole): rib 2, k2tog, yfwd, rib to end.
Work in rib until work measures 15cm (6in), working 2 more buttonholes at 4cm (1½in) intervals.

BUTTONBAND

Work as buttonhole band, omitting buttonholes.

MAKING UP

Using cotton yarn only, join shoulder seams. Join cast-off edge of sleeve between markers. Join side and sleeve seams. Sew buttonbands to front opening. Sew collar to neck, ensuring it covers both ends of bands. Sew on buttons.

SQUARE DANCE JUMPER

Brightly coloured blocks dance across this shawl-collared jumper, which can be knitted in virtually any colour combination. It will look good on both men and women and is knitted using the intarsia method (see p. 8).

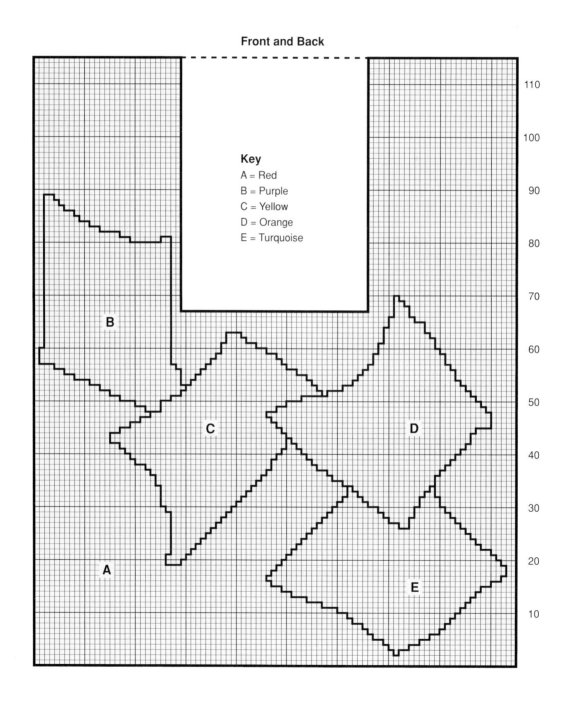

Front and Back

Key
A = Red
B = Purple
C = Yellow
D = Orange
E = Turquoise

SIZE To fit bust/chest **small** (86–92cm/34–36in); **medium** (96–102cm/38–40in); **large** (107–117cm/42–46in). Actual sizes: **small** 107cm (42in) bust/chest, 60cm (23½in) long; **medium** 117cm (46in) bust/chest, 65cm (25½in) long; **large** 135cm (53in) bust/chest, 71cm (28in) long.

MATERIALS Melinda Coss Mohair: Red (A) 450gm, Purple (B) 50gm, Yellow (C) 50gm, Orange (D) 50gm, Turquoise (E) 50gm.

NEEDLES The size of the jumper can be adjusted by using larger or smaller needles: **small** – one pair of 4½mm (no. 7) needles and one pair of 5mm (no. 6) needles: **medium** – one pair of 4½mm (no. 7) needles and one pair of 5½mm (no. 5) needles; **large** – one pair of 5mm (no. 6) needles and one pair of 6mm (no. 4) needles.

TENSION Using 5mm (no. 6) needles and measured over st st, 18 sts and 22 rows = 10cm square (4in square); using 5½mm (no. 5) needles and measured over st st, 16 sts and 20 rows = 10cm square (4in square); using 6mm (no. 4) needles and measured over st st, 14 sts and 18 rows = 10cm square (4in square).

BACK

Using smaller needle size and A, cast on 85 sts.
Work in k1, p1 rib for 7.5cm (3in), inc 10 sts evenly across last row of rib (95 sts).
Change to larger needle size and, working in st st, beg to follow chart, working straight to row 115.
Cast off 29 sts, mark with coloured thread, cast off 37 sts, mark with coloured thread, cast off rem 29 sts.

FRONT

Work as for back until row 67. Work 29 sts, cast off 37 sts, work 29 sts. Continuing to work each side separately, cont to follow the chart until row 115.
Cast off rem 29 sts on each side.

SLEEVES

(Both alike.) Using smaller needle size and A, cast on 38 sts.
Work in k1, p1 rib for 7.5cm (3in), inc 18 sts evenly across last row of rib (56 sts).
Change to larger needle size and, working in st st, beg to follow appropriate sleeve chart, inc 1 st each end of the third row and the 13 foll sixth rows (84 sts). Work 6 rows and cast off loosely.

COLLAR

Using 4½mm (no. 7) needles and A, cast on 142 sts. Work in k1, p1 rib for 19cm (7½in). Rib for 3 more rows. Cast off in rib using 5½mm (no. 5) needles.

MAKING UP

Use backstitch to join the shoulder, arm and side seams, taking care to pull the underarm sleeve seams down to avoid puckering. Sew the collar into position, crossing the front left over right.

19

Right Sleeve

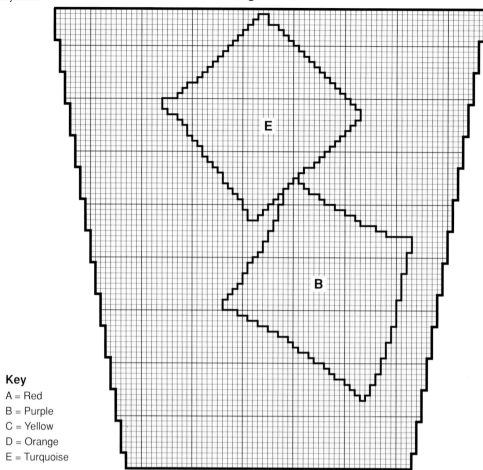

Key
A = Red
B = Purple
C = Yellow
D = Orange
E = Turquoise

Left Sleeve

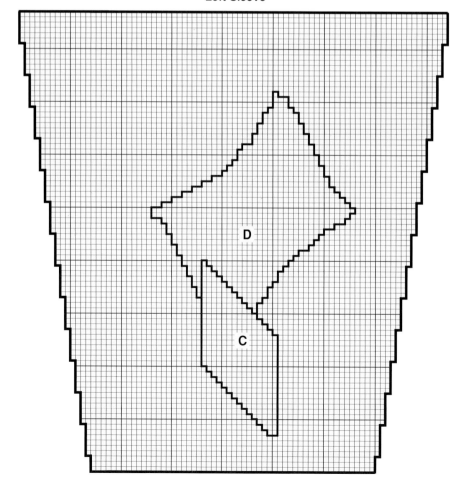

FOUR-NIGHT KNIT JUMPER

This is the perfect 'first knit' for beginners and produces a shape that covers all sins. Worked on large needles, it can be knitted in one colour or in bold bumble-bee stripes. It was christened the 'four-night knit' because that is how long it should take the average knitter to complete! Looks great worn over leggings.

SIZE To fit bust 86–107cm (34–42in). Actual size: 78cm (31in) long.

MATERIALS Melinda Coss Mohair: Black (main colour) 275gm, contrast 160gm.

NEEDLES One pair of 5½mm (no. 5) needles and one pair of 8mm (no. 0) needles. Stitch holder.

TENSION Using 8mm (no. 0) needles and measured over st st, 12 sts and 12 rows = 10cm square (4in square).

NB The body of the jumper is knitted in one piece. The ribs, collar and cuffs are knitted in black. The stripes are knitted over 12 rows, except for the eighth stripe, which forms the shoulder line and is knitted over 15 rows.

FRONT AND BACK

Using 5½mm (no. 5) needles and black, cast on 60 sts. Work in k1, p1 rib until rib measures 18cm (7in).
Change to 8mm (no. 0) needles and, using contrast colour and st st, begin stripe sequence, inc 1 st each end of every alt row until you have 130 sts on your needle. Cont in pattern, work 19 rows without shaping. (You should finish on a purl row in the middle of the black shoulder stripe.) Then **shape neck.**
Knit 50 sts. Place these on a spare needle. Cast off centre 30 sts, knit 50 sts.
Working on these last 50 sts only, purl to last 2 sts, p2tog.
Next row: k2tog, knit to end.
Next row: purl to last st, inc by 1 in last st.
Next row: inc 1, knit to end.
Purl back to neck edge, turn, cast on 30 sts, break off yarn.
Rejoin yarn at neck edge of stitches held on spare needle and work as follows.
Next row: p2tog, purl to end.
Next row: knit to last 2 sts, k2 tog.
Next row: inc 1, purl to end.
Next row: knit to last st, inc 1.
Purl 1 row.
Knit across the 130 sts on both needles, continue down the back exactly as you have knitted the front, but dec where you have inc until you have 60 sts on your needles.

Change to 5½mm (no. 5) needles and black, k1, p1, rib for 18cm (7in).

COLLAR
Using 8mm (no. 0) needles, cast on 74 sts. Work in k1, p1 rib until work measures 23cm (9in). Cast off very loosely.

CUFFS
Using 5½mm (no. 5) needles, cast on 35 sts. Work in k1, p1 rib for 5cm (2in). Inc 1 st each end of next and every alt row until you have 55 sts. Cast off.

MAKING UP
Join side seams and cuff seams, and join short ends of neckband. Stitch cuffs into place and sew on neckband, making sure that the seam is at the centre back.

ANEMONE JACKET

The flower motifs on this boxy, shawl-collared jacket are knitted using the fairisle method (see p. 9) to give a slightly raised effect. Our charcoal grey mohair is especially soft and slightly flecked, giving a lovely muted background to the vibrant anemone colours.

SIZE To fit bust 82–96cm (32–38in), fitting loosely. Actual size: 126cm (50in) bust; 69cm (27in) long; 53cm (20³/₄in) sleeve.

MATERIALS Melinda Coss Mohair: main colour 500gm; Black, Jade, Turquoise, Mid Blue, Royal, Mauve, Fuchsia, Scarlet, Crimson, Emerald, 30gm of each. 3 buttons.

NEEDLES One pair of 5mm (no. 6) needles and one pair of 5¹/₂mm (no. 5) needles. 2 spare needles.

TENSION Using 5¹/₂mm (no. 6) needles and measured over st st, 16 sts and 20 rows = 10cm square (4in square).

NB When working from the charts strand the yarn not in use loosely across the WS of the work to prevent puckering, weaving strands in every 2 or 3 sts to avoid long floats.

BACK

Using 5mm (no. 6) needles and main colour, cast on 100 sts. Work in moss stitch as follows:

Row 1 (RS): (k1, p1) rep to end.
Row 2: (p1, k1) rep to end.
Rep last 2 rows twice more (6 rows worked).
Change to 5¹/₂mm (no. 5) needles and, continuing in main colour and starting with a knit row, work straight in st st until back measures 7cm (2³/₄in) from cast-on edge, ending with a WS row.
Then **place motifs.**
Row 1 (RS): k2 in main colour, work across the 40 sts of first row of chart 1, k58 in main colour.
Row 2: p58 in main colour, work second row of chart 1, p2 in main colour.
Continue to work chart 1 in position as set until 24th row has been worked.
Row 25 (RS): k2 in main colour, work 25th row of chart 1, k13 in main colour, work across 40 sts of first row of chart 2, k5 in main colour.
Next row: p5 in main colour, work 40 sts of second row of chart 2, p13 in main colour, work across 40 sts of 26th row of chart 1, p2 in main colour.
Cont working charts 1 and 2 in positions as set.
When chart 1 is complete, work in main colour, cont to work chart 2 until the 44th row has been worked, ending on a WS row. **Shape armholes.**
Next row: cast off 8 sts, knit to end.
Next row: cast off 8 sts, purl to end (84 sts).

Work 6 rows in st st and main colour.
Next row (RS): k5 in main colour, work across the 40 sts of first row of chart 1, k39 in main colour.
Next row: p39 in main colour, work across 40 sts of second row of chart 1, p5 in main colour. The chart is now placed. Cont straight until the 36th row of the chart has been worked, then cont in main colour only. Work 2 rows in st st (ending with a WS row), then **shape shoulders.**
Cast off 8 sts at beg of next 6 rows. Cast off rem 36 sts for back neck.

POCKET BACKS

(Make 2.) Using 5¹/₂mm

Chart 1

40 sts

Key

☐ = Main colour	● = Turquoise	+ = Fuchsia	
■ = Black	O = Mid Blue	◤ = Crimson	
✕ = Jade	– = Royal	V = Scarlet	
╱ = Emerald	I = Mauve		

Chart 2

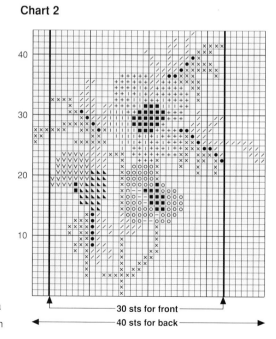

30 sts for front
40 sts for back

(no. 5) needles and main colour, cast on 24 sts. Beg with a knit row and cont in st st for 12cm (4³/₄in), ending with a RS row. Leave sts on a spare needle.

LEFT FRONT

Using 5mm (no. 6) needles and main colour, cast on 52 sts and work in moss st as for back welt for 6 rows. Change to 5¹/₂mm (no. 5) needles and, starting with a knit row, work 4 rows in st st in main colour. Make **pocket top.**
Next row (RS): using main colour, k12, (p1, k1) rep to last 16 sts, k16.
Next row: p16, (k1, p1) to last 12 sts, p12.
Rep last 2 rows 6 times more (14 rows of moss st worked) then **place pocket.**
Next row (RS): k12, cast off 24 sts, k16.
Next row: p16, purl across the 24 sts held on spare needle for pocket back, p12 (52 sts).
Now cont straight across all sts until front measures 30cm (11³/₄in) from cast-on edge, ending with a WS row. **Place motif.**
Next row: k14 in main colour, work across the 30 sts of first row of chart 2, k8 in main colour.
Next row: p8 in main colour, work across second row of chart 2, p14 in main colour. Cont to work straight with the chart in position as set until the front measures the same as the back to the armhole shaping, ending with a WS row. **Shape armhole.**
Keeping chart correct, cast off 8 sts at beg of next row (44 sts).
Cont straight, following chart until 25th row has been worked, ending at neck edge. Keeping chart correct, **shape front neck.**
Dec 1 st at beg (neck edge) on next row and at this edge on every foll alt row until 29 sts rem.
After completing chart, cont in main colour only.
Cont straight in main colour until front measures the same as back to start of shoulder shaping, ending at armhole edge. **Shape shoulder.**
Cast off 8 sts at beg of next row and 2 foll alt rows. Work 1 row. Cast off rem 5 sts.

RIGHT FRONT

Work as for left front, reversing pocket, armhole, neck and shoulder shapings. Also read chart 2 in reverse by reading odd-numbered rows as purl rows and even-numbered rows as knit rows.

SLEEVES

(Both alike.) Using 5¹/₂mm (no. 6) needles and main colour, cast on 54 sts and work in k1, p1 rib for 18cm (7¹/₄in). Starting with a knit row and with main colour, work in st st for 3 rows.
Next row: inc 1 st at each end (56 sts).
Work 2 rows in st st then **place motif.**
Next row (RS): k8 in main colour, work across 40 sts of first row of chart 1, k8 in main colour.
Cont to follow chart 1 in position as set, at the same time inc 1 st at each end of the next row and every foll fourth row until there are 80 sts. When chart is complete work in main colour only.
Work straight until sleeve measures 53cm (20³/₄in) from cast-on edge, ending with a WS row. Cast off loosely. Join shoulder seams.

BUTTONBAND AND HALF COLLAR

Using 5mm (no. 6) needles and main colour, cast on 18 sts. Work in k1, p1 rib until band, slightly stretched, reaches to start of left front neck shaping (sew in position as you work), ending at shaped neck edge of front. Then **shape collar.**
Next row (RS): rib 2 sts, (k1, p1, k1) into next st, rib to end.
Rib 3 rows.
Rep the last 4 rows 11 times in all (40 sts). Now cont straight in rib until band reaches to centre of back neck. Cast off loosely ribwise. Mark on this band the positions of 3 buttons, the first 10cm (4in) up from cast-on edge, the third at the beg of the next shaping, the other midway between.

BUTTONHOLD BAND

Work as for buttonband but make buttonholes when marked positions are reached as follows.
First buttonhole row (RS): rib 7 sts, cast off 4 sts, rib to end.
Next row: rib, casting on 4 sts over cast-off sts on previous row. Reverse shapings on collar.

MAKING UP

Join centre back seam on collar neatly. Join side seams and sew in sleeves. Stitch down sides and bottom edges of pocket backs. Sew on buttons to correspond to buttonholes. Turn up cuffs on the sleeves.

SLIPSTITCH JUMPER

I love slipstitch – it is so easy and looks so difficult. Basically, you knit every row and, in this case, I have changed colours every few rows to give a shaded effect. This is a good jumper for him or her, and it is perfect for beginners.

SIZE To fit bust/chest (small) 86–97cm (34–38in) and (large) 97–112cm (38–44in). Actual size: 103.5cm (41in) and 110cm (43½in) bust/chest; 68cm (27in) long; 53cm (21in) sleeve.

MATERIALS Melinda Coss Mohair: Chocolate/Navy (A) 325gm, Peach/Azure (B) 90gm, Fawn/Mid Blue (C) 75gm, Coffee/Turquoise (D) 65gm, Old Gold/Emerald (E) 60gm, Gingy/Jade (F) 70gm, Chestnut/Royal (G) 65gm.

NEEDLES One pair of 4½mm (no. 7) needles and one pair 6mm (no. 4) needles.

TENSION Using 6mm (no. 4) needles and measured over pattern, 17 sts and 26 rows = 10cm square (4in square).

PATTERN

Row 1 (RS): using A, knit.
Row 2: using A, k3,*k1 wrapping yarn twice round needle, k4, repeat from * to last 3 sts, k3.
Row 3: using B, k3,* slip 1 with yarn at back, dropping extra wrap, k4, repeat from * to last 3 sts, k3.
Row 4: using B, k3,* slip 1 with yarn at front, k4, repeat from * to last 3 sts, k3.
Row 5: repeat row 3.
Row 6: repeat row 4.
Repeat the last 6 rows once more.
These 12 rows form the pattern. Continue repeating them throughout, but change the contrast colour every 12 rows from B to C to D to E to F and then to G (60 rows after first set of 12 are complete). Then repeat sequence again from beg for a further 72 rows. Then work 12 rows of pattern, once more using contrast B. Cast off all sts.

BACK

Using 4½mm (no. 7) needles and A, cast on 88/94 sts. Work in k1, p1 rib for 8cm (3in) inc 10/14 sts evenly across last row (98/108 sts).
Change to 6mm (no. 4) needles and work in pattern as described * for 156 rows. Cast off all sts.

FRONT

Work as for back to *. Then cont in pattern for 72 rows. **Shape neck.**

Work 35 sts. Cast off 38 sts. Work 35 sts. Continue working both sides of neck in pattern until front matches back to shoulder.

SLEEVES

(Both alike.) Using 4½mm (no. 7) needles and A, cast on 34/38 sts. Work in k1, p1 rib for 8cm (3in).
Change to 6mm (no. 4) needles and begin working in pattern, inc 1 st each end of every fifth row until you have 90 sts. Work straight until sleeve measures approx 42cm (16½in) including rib, or to desired length, finishing on a row 1 or row 7 of pattern sequence. Cast off.

COLLAR

Using 4½mm (no. 7) needles and A, cast on 140 sts. Work in single rib for 20cm (7¾in). Cast off.

MAKING UP

Join sleeves to body, then join side seams. Attach collar with cast-off edge to the neckline, and then cross right front over left and slipstitch short end along front of neck edge.

SHELL JACKET AND COAT

Rainbow colours permeate this easily worked jacket and coat set. The simple motif repeat is worked using the fairisle method (see p.9) and the shaded colour sequence makes this design both versatile and flattering.

SIZE To fit bust 86–107cm (34–42in). Actual size: 138cm (54in) from edge to edge; jacket 77cm (30in) long, coat 110cm (43in) long; 48cm (19in) sleeve.

MATERIALS Melinda Coss Mohair: Black (A) 450(570)gm, Emerald (B), Turquoise (C), Royal (D), Purple (E), Mauve (F), Fuchsia (G), 75gm of each. Coat only: Scarlet (H), Orange (J), Yellow (L), 75gm of each.

NEEDLES One pair of 4½mm (no. 7) needles and one pair of 5½mm (no. 5) needles.

TENSION Using 5½mm (no. 5) needles and measured over shell pattern, 18 sts and 18 rows = 10cm square (4in square).

NB When working the colour pattern, strand the yarn not in use loosely across the WS to prevent puckering, weaving strands in after 2 or 3 stitches to avoid long floats.

BACK

Using 5½mm (no. 5) needles and A, cast on 109 sts. Beg with a knit row, work in st st, foll pattern from chart 1 and using key 1, as follows.
Row 1: work first row of chart 1, rep the 12 sts before the dotted line until last st. Knit the st beyond the dotted line.
Row 2: purl the stitch before the dotted line and repeat the 12 sts beyond the dotted line to end of row.
Cont in this way, working the 20 rows of chart 1.
Using key 2, rep chart 1 once more. Then cont to rep chart 1, using colours in order as follows: key 3, key 4, key 5, key 6 (coat only: key 7, key 8 and key 9).
Cast off loosely in A.

LEFT FRONT

Using 5½mm (no. 5) needles and A, cast on 9 sts. Beg with a knit row, work in st st, foll pattern from chart 2, ignoring the dotted lines, and using key 1 as follows.
Row 1: beg level with Y, k9.
Row 2: cast on 8 and, following the second row of chart 2, p17.*
Cont in this way, casting on 6 sts at the beg of next and foll alt rows, 4 sts at beg of next alt row, 3 sts at beg of next alt row and 2 sts at beg of next alt row as shown on chart 2, ending with 13th row of chart.

Cont in pattern as set, inc 1 st at shaped edge on next 12 rows and changing colours to key 2 after row 20 has been worked. Then cont to inc 1 st at this edge on foll 5 alt rows (55 sts). Cont straight in colours as back until the ninth row of the fourth (seventh) pattern from the beg has been worked.** **Shape front.**
Dec 1 st at shaped edge of next and every foll alt row until 37 sts rem. Cont straight until (sixth) ninth pattern from beg has been worked. Cast off loosely in A.

RIGHT FRONT

Using 5½mm (no. 5) needles and A, cast on 9 sts. Beg with a knit row, work in st st, foll pattern from chart 2 within area marked by dotted lines and reading RS (odd-numbered) rows from left to right and WS (even-numbered) rows from right to left.
Use key 1 as follows.
Row 1: beg level with Z, k9.
Row 2: p9 to dotted line.
Row 3: cast on 8 sts shown by dotted line and, following third row of chart 2, k17.
Working within the dotted lines of chart 2, work as for left front from *, reversing front shaping from ** by dec at the end, not the beg, of rows.

SLEEVES

(Both alike.) Using 4½mm (no. 7) needles and A, cast on 70 sts. Work in k2, p2 rib for 15cm (6in), inc 1 st each end and at centre of last row (73 sts).
Change to 5½mm (no. 5) needles and, beginning with a knit row, work pattern from chart 1 as given for back, using colours in order of key 4, key 5 and key 6 for jacket (key 7, key 8 and key 9 for coat), **at the same time** inc 1 st each end of the third and every foll fourth row, taking made sts into pattern at each side, until there are 97 sts. Cont straight until third pattern from beg has been worked. Cast off loosely in A.

MAKING UP

Join the shoulder seams. Beginning and ending 27cm (10½in) from shoulder seams, sew on sleeves. Join the side and sleeve seams.
Border: using 4½mm (no. 7) needles and A, cast on 22 sts. Work in k2, p2 rib until work is long enough to fit around entire outer edge, beginning and ending at centre of cast-off edge of back neck and allowing sufficient ease to keep border flat around front curves. Sew on border and join ends.

Right Front

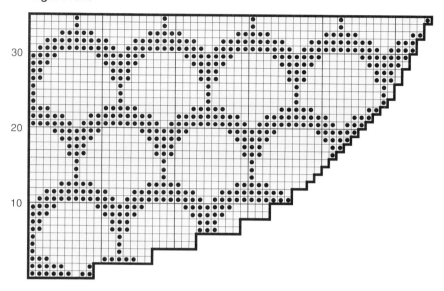

Left Front

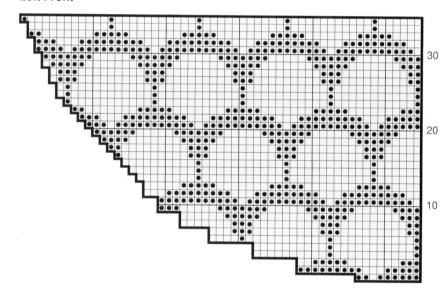

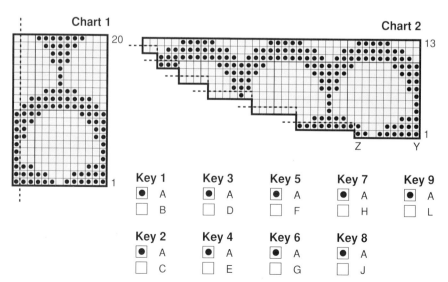

Chart 1

Chart 2

Key 1	Key 3	Key 5	Key 7	Key 9
● A	● A	● A	● A	● A
☐ B	☐ D	☐ F	☐ H	☐ L

Key 2	Key 4	Key 6	Key 8
● A	● A	● A	● A
☐ C	☐ E	☐ G	☐ J

FLASH ARROWS JUMPER

This big batwing jumper with its rainbow stripes can be worn with virtually anything. A good design for beginners, and wonderfully comfortable to wear.

SIZE To fit bust 92–112cm (36–44in). Actual size: 148cm (58in) from cuff to cuff; 80cm (31$\frac{1}{2}$in) long.

MATERIALS Melinda Coss Mohair: Black (A) 500gm, Emerald (B) 25gm, Turquoise (C) 25gm, Royal (D) 30gm, Mid Blue (E) 35gm, Purple (F) 30gm, Mauve (G) 30gm, Fuchsia (H) 25gm, Scarlet (J) 25gm, Orange (K) 25gm, Yellow (L) 25gm.

NEEDLES One pair of 4$\frac{1}{2}$mm (no. 7) needles, one pair of long 5$\frac{1}{2}$mm (no. 5) needles (or, if preferred, use a 5$\frac{1}{2}$mm (no. 5) circular needle for working backwards and forwards in rows) and one 4$\frac{1}{2}$mm (no. 7) circular needle, 60cm (24in) long. Stitch holders.

TENSION Using 5$\frac{1}{2}$mm (no. 5) needles and measured over pattern, 16 sts and 20 rows = 10cm square (4in square).

NB Use separate balls of yarn for each contrast colour each side of the centre V, carrying the black across, and twist yarns together at the back of your work when changing colours to avoid making a hole.

FRONT

Using 4$\frac{1}{2}$mm (no. 7) needles and A, cast on 95 sts.
Rib row 1 (RS): k1, (p1, k1) to end.
Rib row 2: p1, (k1, p1) to end.
Rep these 2 rows for 15cm (6in), ending with a row 2 and inc 6 sts evenly across the last row (101 sts).
Change to 5$\frac{1}{2}$mm (no. 5) needles and, beg with a knit row, work in st st and stripe pattern as follows.
Row 1: k32A, k5B, k8A, k5C, k1A, k5C, k8A, k5B, k32A.
Row 2: p31A, p5B, p8A, p5C, p3A, p5C, p8A, p5B, p31A.
Row 3: k30A, k5B, k8A, k5C, k5A, k5C, k8A, k5B, k30A.
Row 4: p29A, p5B, p8A, p5C, p7A, p5C, p8A, p5B, p29A.
Rows 5–8: cont as set, moving stripes by 1 st and working 2 more sts in A in centre V on each row.
Row 9: k24A, k5B, k8A, k5C, k8A, k1D, k8A, k5C, k8A, k5B, k24A.
Row 10: p23A, p5B, p8A, p5C, p8A, p3D, p8A, p5C, p8A, p5B, p23A.
Rows 11–13: cont as set, moving stripes by 1 st and working 2 more sts in D in centre V on each row.
Row 14: p19A, p5B, p8A, p5C, p8A, p5D, p1A, p5D, p8A, p5C, p8A, p5B, p19A.
Rows 15–21: cont as set, moving stripes by 1 st and working 2 more sts in A in centre V on each row.

Work in pattern, introducing new colours on given rows and working 2 more sts in appropriate colour in centre V as follows.
Row 22: p11A, p5B, p8A, p5C, p8A, p5D, p1E, p8A, p5D, p8A, p5C, p8A, p5B, p11A.
Rows 23–26: work in pattern as set.
Row 27: k6A, k5B, k8A, k5C, k8A, k5D, k8A, k5E, k1A, k5E, k8A, k5D, k8A, k5C, k8A, k5B, k6A.
Rows 28–30: work 3 rows straight.
Sleeve shaping: cont in pattern and inc 1 st each end of next and foll alt row (105 sts). Work 1 row straight.
Row 35: inc in first st, work pattern for 51 sts, k1F, work pattern for 51 sts, inc in last st. Cont to inc 1 st at each end of every RS row, introducing new colours on given rows as follows.
Rows 36–39: work pattern as set.
Row 40: work pattern for 55 sts, p1A, work pattern for 55 sts.
Rows 41–47: work pattern as set.
Row 48: work pattern for 59 sts, p1G, work pattern for 59 sts.
Rows 49–52: work pattern as set.
Row 53: inc in first st, work pattern for 60 sts, k1A, work pattern for 60 sts, inc in last st.
Rows 54–60: work pattern as set.
Row 61: inc in first st, work pattern for 64 sts, k1H, work pattern for 64 sts, inc in last st (133 sts).
Rows 62–65: work pattern as set.
Row 66: work pattern for 68 sts, p1A, work pattern for 68 sts.
Rows 67–73: work pattern as set.
Row 74: work pattern for 72 sts, p1J, work pattern for 72 sts.
Rows 75–78: work pattern as set, inc on RS rows (149 sts). Inc 1 st at each end of every row and cont to introduce new colours as follows.
Row 79: inc in first st, work pattern for 73 sts, k1A, work pattern for 73 sts, inc in last st.
Rows 80–86: work pattern as set.
Row 87: inc in first st, work pattern for 81 sts, k1K, work pattern for 81 sts, inc in last st.
Rows 88–91: work pattern as set.
Row 92: inc in first st, work pattern for 86 sts, p1A, work pattern for 86 sts, inc in last st.
Rows 93–99: work pattern as set.
Row 100: inc in first st, work pattern for 94 sts, p1L, work pattern for 94 sts, inc in last st.
Rows 101–104: work pattern as set.
Row 105: inc in first st, work pattern for 99 sts, k1A, work pattern for 99 sts, inc in last st.
Row 106: inc in first st, work pattern for 201 sts, inc in last st (205 sts).
Place markers at each end of the last row.
Work 10 rows straight, cont to move stripes and working 2 sts more in A in centre V on each row. **Shape neck.**

Next row: work pattern for 92 sts, turn and work on this set of sts only. Cont in pattern, dec 1 st at neck edge on next 10 rows (82 sts). Work 3 rows straight and cast off in pattern.
With RS facing, slip centre 21 sts on a holder, join A to next st and work pattern to end. Complete to match first side.

BACK
Work as front to cast-off row, omitting neck shaping.
Next row: using appropriate colours, cast off 82 sts, break off yarn, slip next 41 sts on a holder, join yarn to next st and cast off rem 82 sts.

MAKING UP
Join both shoulder seams, matching the stripes.
Collar: using a 4½mm (no. 7) circular needle and A and with RS facing, beg at left shoulder seam and pick up and knit 134 sts around neck edge, inc those on holders. Work in rounds of k1, p1 rib for 22cm (8½in). Cast off loosely in rib.
Cuffs: using 4½mm (no. 7) needles and A and with RS facing, pick up and knit 48 sts along row ends of sleeves between markers. Purl 1 row, dec 7 sts (41 sts). Beg with rib row 1, work 10cm (4in) in rib as for front welt. Cast off in rib. Matching the stripes, join the side and sleeve seams.

DOGTOOTH COAT

This fairisled three-quarter-length coat is both smart and elegant. It has been knitted up in a multitude of colour combinations. Clear contrasts work best, and next to the classic red and black I favour a combination of yellow and black.

SIZE To fit bust 86–107cm (34–42in). Actual size: 136cm (53½in) bust; 94cm (37in) long; approximately 47.5cm (19in) sleeve with cuff turned back.

MATERIALS Melinda Coss Mohair: Black (A) 525gm and contrast colour (B) 325gm. 6 buttons.

NEEDLES One pair of 4½mm (no. 7) needles and one pair of 5½mm (no. 5) needles.

TENSION Using 5½mm (no. 5) needles and measured over pattern, 16 sts and 16 rows = 10cm square (4in square).

NB When working the pattern from the chart, strand the yarn not in use loosely across the WS of the work to prevent puckering and weave strands in after every 2 or 3 stitches to avoid long floats.

BACK

Using 4½mm (no. 7) needles and A, cast on 92 sts. Work in k1, p1 rib for 6.5cm (2½in).
Next row: rib 5, (inc in next st, rib 8) rep to last 6 sts, inc in next st, rib to end (102 sts).
Change to 5½mm (no. 5) needles and, working in st st throughout, follow pattern from chart until back measures 66.5cm (26¼in) from cast-on edge, ending with a purl row. **Shape armholes.**
Keeping pattern correct throughout, cast off 9 sts at beg of next 2 rows (84 sts). Work straight until back measures 94cm (37in) from cast-on edge, ending with a purl row. **Shape shoulders.**
Cast off 8 sts at beg of next 6 rows. Cast off rem 36 sts, placing a marker 5 sts in from each end to indicate back neck.

LEFT FRONT

Using 4½mm (no. 7) needles and A, cast on 46 sts. Work in k1, p1 rib for 6.5cm (2½in).
Next row: rib 5, (inc in next st, rib 8) rep to last 5 sts, inc in next st, rib to end (51 sts).
Change to 5½mm (no. 5) needles and, working in st st throughout, follow pattern from chart until front measures the same as back to beg of armhole shaping, ending with a purl row (for right front, end with a knit row here). **Shape armhole.**
Keeping pattern correct throughout, cast off 9 sts at beg of next

row (42 sts). Work 4 rows. **Shape front.**
Dec 1 st at beg of next and foll alt row until 29 sts rem. Work straight until front measures same as back to beg of shoulder shaping, ending at the armhole edge. **Shape shoulders.**
Cast off 8 sts at beg of next and foll 2 alt rows. Cast off rem 5 sts.

RIGHT FRONT

Work as for left front but noting bracketed exception.

SLEEVES

(Both alike.) Using 5½mm (no. 5) needles and A, cast on 51 sts.
Rib row 1: k1, (p1, k1) to end.
Rib row 2: p1, (k1, p1) to end.
Rep these 2 rows for 16.5cm (6½in), ending with a row 2.
Working in st st throughout, work 3 rows in pattern from the chart. Then, taking extra sts into pattern, inc 1 st each end of next and every foll third row until there are 59 sts, and then at each end of every foll fourth row until there are 85 sts. Work 7 rows straight (ending with chart row 18). Cast off.

POCKETS

(Work 2.) Using 5½mm (no. 5) needles and A, cast on 30 sts.
Working in st st throughout, work 27 rows in pattern from chart. Change to 4½mm (no. 7) needles and, working in A only, work in k1, p1 rib for 4 rows. Cast off in rib.

BUTTONBAND AND LEFT COLLAR

Using 5½mm (no. 5) needles and A, cast on 18 sts. Work in k1, p1 rib until the band, slightly stretched, fits up the front edge to the beg of front shaping.
Shape collar.
Next row (RS): rib 2, inc 2, rib to end.
Rows 2–4: rib to end.
Rep last 4 rows 12 times more.
Next row: rib 2, inc 2, rib to end (46 sts)
Work straight until band, slightly stretched, fits up front edge to centre back neck. Cast off in rib.
Mark positions for 6 buttons, the first 3cm (1¼in) from cast-on

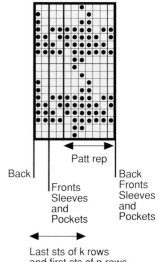

Patt rep

Back | Back
Fronts | Fronts
Sleeves | Sleeves
and | and
Pockets | Pockets

Last sts of k rows
and first sts of p rows

Key

□ = A (Black)

▣ = B (contrast colour)

edge and the last 2cm (³/₄in) from beg of the collar shaping, the remainder spaced evenly between.

BUTTONHOLE BAND AND RIGHT COLLAR
Work as for buttonband and left collar, reversing the direction of shaping by reading WS row for RS row. Work buttonholes to correspond with markers as follows.
Buttonhole row 1 (RS): rib 7, cast off 4, rib to end.

Buttonhole row 2: rib, casting on 4 sts over those cast off on previous row.

MAKING UP
Join the shoulder seams. Set in the sleeves then join the side and sleeve seams. Sew each front band and collar into position and sew cast-off edges together at centre back neck. Sew on the pockets and buttons.

HARLEQUIN COAT

We have it on good authority that this three-quarter-length coat stops the traffic. It should be knitted using the intarsia method (see p. 8).

> **SIZE** To fit bust 86–96cm (34–38in). Actual size: 131cm (52in) bust; 82cm (32in) long; 47cm (19in) sleeve.
>
> **MATERIALS** Melinda Coss Mohair: Black (A) 375gm, Royal (B) 60gm, Turquoise (C) 75gm, Orange (D) 30gm, Candyfloss (E) 75gm, Yellow (F) 75gm, Emerald (G) 30gm, Scarlet (H) 50gm. 1 button.
>
> **NEEDLES** One pair of 5mm (no. 6) needles and one pair of 5½mm (no. 5) needles.
>
> **TENSION** Using 5½mm (no. 5) needles and measured over st st, 16 sts and 19 rows = 10cm square (4in square).

BACK

Using 5mm (no. 6) needles and A, cast on 105 sts. Beg with a knit row, work 7 rows in st st. Knit 1 row to mark the hemline. Change to 5½mm (no. 5) needles and, working in st st, beg to follow the chart, reading every row from right to left.
Row 1 (RS): k1B, k25A, k1C, k25A, k1D, k25A, k1E, k25A, k1C (for edge st).
This row sets the pattern. Work the colour sequence from the colour plan, noting that colours in brackets refer to left and right

fronts only. Cont as set, working the 26-st pattern rep 4 times and the edge st once, until the 26 rows of the chart have been worked 6 times in all. Cast off.

LEFT FRONT

Using 5mm (no. 6) needles and A, cast on 53 sts. Beg with a knit row, work 7 rows in st st. Knit 1 row to mark the hemline. Change to 5½mm (no. 5) needles.** Work in st st in colour sequence, foll colour plan for left front. Where two colours are given, use the colour in brackets. Work from chart as follows.
Row 1 (RS): k1C, k25A, k1E, k25A, k1D (for edge st).
Cont as set until 139 pattern rows have been worked, ending with the ninth row of the sixth line of triangles. **Shape neck.** Cont in pattern, cast off 10 sts at beg of next row, then dec 1 st at neck edge on foll 6 rows (37 sts). Work straight until chart has been worked 6 times in all. Cast off.

RIGHT FRONT

Work as for left front to **. Complete to match left front, following colour plan for right front and working 1 more row before neck shaping.

LEFT SLEEVE

With 5mm (no. 6) needles and A, cast on 49 sts. Work in moss st as follows.

Colour plan

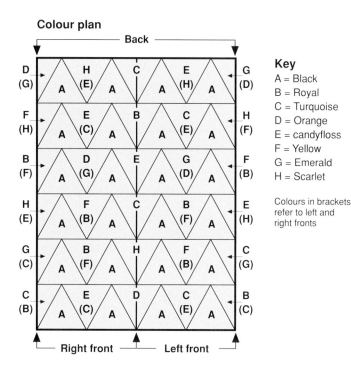

Key
A = Black
B = Royal
C = Turquoise
D = Orange
E = candyfloss
F = Yellow
G = Emerald
H = Scarlet

Colours in brackets refer to left and right fronts

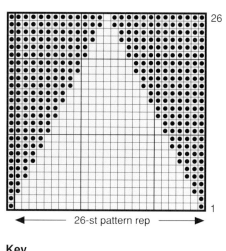

Key
☐ = Black   ⦿ = Contrast colour as given in pattern

Next row: p1, * k1, p1, rep from * to end.
Rep this row for 12cm (4¾in). Change to 5½mm (no. 5) needles and work in st st in pattern as follows.
Row 1: k24A, k1F, k24A. This row sets the position of the first F triangle. Keeping the pattern correct and working all increases in A, inc 1 st each end of second and every foll third row until there are 65 sts. Work last row of chart with no inc.
Row 27: using A, inc in first st, k5A, k1E, k25A, k1B, k25A, k1H, k5A, inc in last st using A. This row sets the position and colour sequence for the second row of triangles. Work a further 25 rows (83 sts).
Row 53: k15A, k1H, k25A, k1C, k25A, k1E, k15A. This row sets the position and colour sequence for the third row of triangles. Work a further 13 rows (93 sts).
Row 67: k2B, k11A, k15H, k11A, k15C, k11A, k15E, k11A, k2B. Cont as set, working the B triangles into the pattern until there are 99 sts, ending with the 23rd row of the third line of triangles. Work 3 rows straight. Cast off.

RIGHT SLEEVE
Work as for left sleeve but place contrasting triangles as follows.
Line 1: E.
Line 2: G, B and H.
Line 3: E, F and C, then bring F into pattern again at each end of row 67.

FRONT FACINGS
(Work 2.) Using 5mm (no. 6) needles and A and with RSs facing, pick up and knit 127 sts between neck edge and hemline. Beg with a purl row, work 5 rows in st st. Cast off.

MAKING UP
Join shoulder seams, matching triangles. Fold facings to WS and slipstitch in place. **Make the collar.** Using 5mm (no. 6) needles and A and with RSs facing, pick up and knit 23 sts up right front neck edge, 31 sts across back neck and 23 sts down left front neck edge (77 sts).
Inc row: p4, *inc in next st, p3, rep from * until 4 sts rem, p4 (95 sts). Work in moss st as for sleeves until collar measures 5cm (2in). Change to 5½mm (no. 5) needles and moss st for a further 7cm (2¾in). Cast off loosely.
Sew on sleeves. Join side and sleeve seams, reversing 6cm (2½in) of seam on sleeves for cuffs. Turn up hem at hemline and slipstitch into position. Sew on the button at neck edge, making a button loop to correspond.

'Exclusively Yours' coat

There must be something about the shape of diamonds that catches the imagination, since every design I have produced incorporating this motif has proved a huge success. This curved coat works equally well in muted pastels and in bright colours. It is worked using the intarsia method (see p. 8).

SIZE To fit bust 86–102cm (34–40in). Actual size: 150cm (59in) bust; 94cm (37in) long.

MATERIALS Melinda Coss Mohair: Black/Mink (A) 725gm, Yellow/Lemon (B), Turquoise/Mint (C), Fuchsia/Peach (D), Royal/Azure (E), 40gm of each.

NEEDLES One pair of 5¹/₂mm (no. 5) needles.

TENSION Using 5¹/₂mm (no. 5) needles and measured over st st, 16¹/₂ sts and 20 rows = 10cm square (4in square).

NB A separate ball of yarn must be used for each section of black/mink (A) throughout.

BACK

Using 5¹/₂mm (no. 5) needles and A, cast on 112 sts. Beg with a knit row, work 18 rows in st st. Then beg to work first diamond as follows.

Row 1 (RS): k56A, k1B, k55A.
Row 2: p55A, p1B, p56A.
Row 3: k55A, k3B, k54A.
Cont in st st, working diamond from chart until row 35 has been worked. Now set position for second and third diamonds as follows.
Next row: p36A, p1D, p10A, p17B, p10A, p1C, p37A.
Cont as set until B diamond has been completed and row 19 of C and D diamonds has been worked. **Work raglan.**
Keeping C and D diamonds correct, cast off 2 sts at the beg of the next 2 rows, then dec 1 st at each end of the next and every foll alt row until row 33 of C and D diamonds has been worked, ending on a WS row (96 sts).
Set position for fourth diamond as follows.
Next row: using A k2tog, k18A, k19C, k9A, k1E, k9A, k19D, k17A, using A k2tog.
Next row: p18A, p19D, p9A, p1E, p9A, p19C, p19A.
Continuing to dec each end of alt rows as before, complete C, D and E diamonds.
Still dec on alt rows, cont with A only until 18 sts remain. Cast off.

LEFT FRONT

Using 5¹/₂mm (no. 5) needles and A, cast on 8 sts. Beg with a knit row, work in st st, shaping front edge as follows. Work 1 row. * Cast on 7 sts at the beg of the next row, 5 sts at the beg of the foll 2 alt rows, 3 sts at the beg of the next alt row and 2 sts at the beg of the next alt row (30 sts).*

Work 1 row.

Inc 1 st at front edge on next 3 rows, ending with a purl row. Now beg first diamond as follows.

Next row: k16A, k1D, k15A, inc in last st.

Next row: inc in first st, p16A, p1D, p16A.

** Cont to inc 1 st at front edge on every row **and at the same time** complete 17 rows of the first diamond (50 sts).

Inc 1 st at front edge on every foll alt row until row 35 of first diamond has been worked (59 sts).

Now, working front edge straight, set position for second diamond as follows.

Next row: p23A, p1E, p10A, p17D, p8A.

Next row: k8A, k17D, k10A, k1E, k23A.

Cont working the two diamonds until the first diamond is complete, then work 5 more rows, so completing row 23 of second diamond (for right front, work 1 more row here) and ending at side edge. **Shape raglan.**

Keeping diamond correct, cast off 2 sts at beg of next row. Dec 1 st at raglan on every RS row until row 40 of second diamond has been worked, ending with a knit row (49 sts).

Cont to dec at raglan edge on alt rows, dec 1 st at front edge on next and every foll sixth row, working with A only when second diamond is complete, until 2 sts remain. Work 1 row. Work 2 tog and fasten off.**

RIGHT FRONT

Using 5½mm (no. 5) needles and A, cast on 8 sts.

Row 1: knit.

Row 2: purl.

Continue in st st, working as given for left front from * to *.

Inc 1 st at front edge on next 3 rows, ending with a purl row, then set position for first diamond as follows.

Next row: inc in first st, k15A, k1B, k16A.

Next row: p16A, p1B, p16A, inc in last st.

Work as given for left front from ** to **, noting bracketed exception and setting position for second diamond as follows: p8A, p17B, p10A, p1C, p23A.

SLEEVES

(Both alike.) Using 5½mm (no. 5) needles and A, cast on 48 sts.

Knit 4 rows, then work in k6, p6 rib until sleeve measures 12.5cm (5in) from cast-on edge, inc 5 sts evenly across last row (53 sts).

Beg with a knit row, work 6 rows in st st, inc 1 st each end of every row (65 sts).

Cont in st st throughout, set position for first diamond as follows.

Next row: inc in first st, k31A, k1B, k31A, inc in last st (67 sts).

Cont inc 1 st each end of every row until 22 rows of the first diamond are complete (109 sts). Insert a marker at each end of the last row to denote the beg of the armhole. **Shape raglan.**

Keeping diamond correct, work 4 rows straight. Dec 1 st at each end of the next and every foll fourth row until row 35 of

diamond has been worked (103 sts). Set positions for second and third diamonds as follows.

Next row: p32A, p1D, p10A, p17B, p10A, p1C, p32A.

Keeping the three diamonds correct as set, cont to dec on every fourth row until 95 sts remain, then on every foll alt row, **at the same time** completing the first diamond, and then cont until row 33 of the second and third diamonds have been worked (79 sts). Set position for fourth diamond as follows.

Next row: using A k2tog, k9A, k19C, k9A, k1E, k9A, k19D, k9A, using A k2tog.

Cont to dec each end of every alt row, complete the second and third diamonds, then work until row 45 of the fourth diamond is complete (33 sts).

Dec 1 st at each end of the next 5 rows. Insert a marker at the beg of the last row for the right sleeve and at the end of the last row for the left sleeve to denote the top of the front raglan seam. Cont to dec 1 st at each end of every row, completing the fourth diamond. Then continue with A until 11 sts remain. Cast off.

MAKING UP

Join the raglan seams of the back and sleeves, then join each front raglan shaping to the sleeves up to the marker. **Make the border.**

Using 5½mm (no. 5) needles and A, cast on 30 sts.

Row 1 (RS): (k6, p6) twice, k6.

Row 2: (p6, k6) twice, p6.

Rep these 2 rows until the border fits all round the outer edge of the coat, beginning and ending at the centre back neck. Cast off. Sew the border in position, then join the back neck seam.

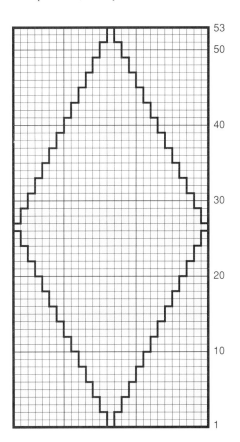

MAN'S GEOMETRIC SWEATER

Something for the boys! A sporty geometric jumper that you should knit for 'him' and immediately borrow back. This also looks wonderful in mink, with pastel-coloured contrasts. Not a difficult one to get to grips with.

SIZE To fit chest 96–102cm (38–40in); for chest size 107–112cm (42–44in) use needles that are half a size larger throughout. Actual size: 114cm (45in) chest; 67cm (26¹/₄in) long.

MATERIALS Melinda Coss Mohair: Navy (Main colour) 450gm, Red (A), Yellow (B), Emerald (C), Silver (D), Royal (E), 40gm of each.

NEEDLES One pair of 4¹/₂mm (no. 7) needles and one pair of 6mm (no. 4) needles.

TENSION Using 6mm (no. 4) needles and measured over st st, 16 sts and 18 rows = 10cm square (4in square).

FRONT

Using 4¹/₂mm (no. 7) needles and main colour, cast on 74 sts. Work in k1, p1 rib for 16 rows, changing colours as desired every 2 rows. Inc 16 sts evenly across last row of rib (90 sts). Change to 6mm (no. 4) needles and, working in st st, beg to follow the chart, working straight until row 108 has been completed.
Row 109 (RS): work 31 sts, cast off 28 sts, work 31 sts. Cont to work each side separately, dec 1 st at the neck edge on the next 6 rows. **At the same time**, when 5 decreases have been completed, shape shoulder by casting off 12 sts at the shoulder edge on the next row and 13 sts on the foll alt row. Rep for other side of neck.

BACK

Work as for front, reading the chart in reverse (i.e., knit rows from left to right and purl rows from right to left) and ignoring the neck shaping.

SLEEVES

(Both alike.) Using 4½mm (no. 7) needles and main colour, cast on 36 sts. Work in k1, p1 rib for 24 rows, changing colours as desired every 2 rows. Inc 14 sts evenly across last row of rib (50 sts).

Change to 6mm (no. 4) needles and, working in st st, beg to follow sleeve chart, inc 1 st each end of every third row 20 times (90 sts). Work without further shaping until 65 rows have been completed (row 90 of chart). Cast off loosely.

NECKBAND

Join one shoulder using flat stitch. With RSs facing, using 4½mm (no. 7) needles and a contrast colour, pick up and knit 7 sts down right side of the front, 28 sts from centre front, 7 sts up left side of front and 40 sts from centre back of neck.

Changing colours as desired every 2 rows, work in k1, p1 rib for 8 rows. Cast off loosely in rib.

MAKING UP

Using main colour, flat-stitch all seams. Fold the neckband in on itself and carefully stitch the cast-off edge to the cast-on edge.

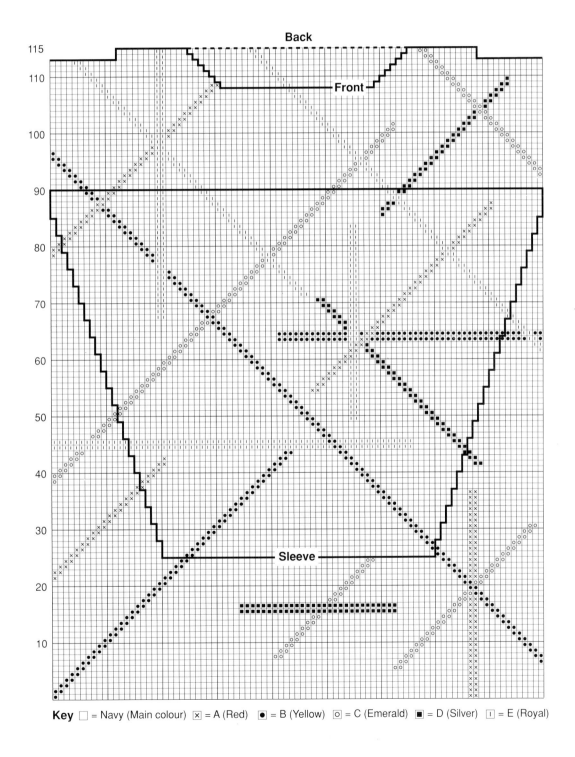

Key ☐ = Navy (Main colour) ☒ = A (Red) ⬤ = B (Yellow) ⊡ = C (Emerald) ■ = D (Silver) ⊟ = E (Royal)

RAZZLE DAZZLE JACKET AND COAT

And you *will* razzle dazzle in this super-bright geometric jacket and coat set. Worked using the intarsia method (see p. 8), it is a good design on which to try out your newly acquired multicolouring skills.

SIZE To fit bust 81–102cm (32–40in). Actual size: 139cm (54³/₄in) bust, jacket 69cm (27in) long, coat 88cm (34¹/₂in) long, 40cm (15³/₄in) sleeve seam.

MATERIALS Melinda Coss Mohair:
JACKET: Black (main colour, MC) 250gm, Orange (A) 65gm, Turquoise (B) 75gm, Scarlet (C) 80gm, Yellow (D) 50gm, Fuchsia (E) 65gm, Emerald (F) 40gm. 7 buttons.
COAT: Black (MC) 335gm, Orange (A) 85gm, Turquoise (B) 95gm, Scarlet (C) 100gm, Yellow (D) 50gm, Fuchsia (E) 65gm, Emerald (F) 40gm. 9 buttons.

NEEDLES One pair of 5mm (no. 6) needles and one pair of 5¹/₂mm (no. 5) needles. Stitch holder. Safety pin.

TENSION Using 5¹/₂mm (no. 5) needles and measured over pattern, 16 sts and 20 rows = 10cm square (4in square).

JACKET

BACK

Using 5mm (no. 6) needles and MC, cast on 102 sts. Work 6 rows in garter st (knit every row).
Next row: knit to end, inc 5 sts evenly across (107 sts).
Change to 5¹/₂mm (no. 5) needles. Beg with a knit row, cont in st st from chart as follows.
Row 1 (RS): reading row 1 of chart from right to left, knit st before dotted line, (k26-st pattern) 4 times, k2 sts beyond dotted line.
Row 2: reading row 2 of chart from left to right, p2 sts before dotted line, (p26-st pattern) 4 times, purl st beyond dotted line.
Cont from chart until all 130 rows have been completed .*
Shape shoulder.
Using MC, cast off 20 sts at beg of next 4 rows. Leave rem 27 sts on a st holder.

LEFT FRONT

Using 5mm (no. 6) needles and MC, cast on 60 sts. Work 6 rows in garter st .**
Next row (WS): k8 and leave these 8 sts on a st holder for buttonband, k9, (inc in next st, k16) twice, inc in next st, k8 (55 sts).
Change to 5¹/₂mm (no. 5) needles. Cont in st st from chart as

back, but work 26-st pattern twice (not 4 times) on each row until row 116 has been completed .*** **Shape neck.**
Next row: pattern to last 6 sts, turn and leave rem 6 sts on a safety pin. Keeping pattern correct, cast off 3 sts at beg of next row, 2 sts on foll alt row and 1 st on next 4 alt rows (40 sts). Pattern 2 rows, ending at side edge with same pattern row as on back. **Shape shoulder.**
Using MC, cast off 20 sts at beg of next row. Work 1 row. Cast off rem 20 sts.

RIGHT FRONT

Work as left front to **.
Next row (WS): k8, (inc in next st, k16) twice, inc in next st, k9, turn and leave rem 8 sts on a st holder for buttonhole band (55 sts) .****
Change to 5¹/₂mm (no. 5) needles. Complete to match left front, ending row 117 before shaping neck. After shaping neck pattern 1 row, knit 1 row in MC before shaping the shoulder.

SLEEVES

(Both alike.) Using 5mm (no. 6) needles and MC, cast on 43 sts. Work 7 rows in garter st.
Next row: purl to end inc 3 sts evenly across (46 sts).
Change to 5¹/₂mm (no. 5) needles. Inc 1 st each end of every third row, cont in st st in stripes of 5 rows B, 5 rows E, 5 rows F, 9 rows MC, 5 rows A, 5 rows B, 5 rows C, 9 rows MC, 5 rows D, 5 rows E, 5 rows F and 9 rows MC (94 sts). Cast off loosely with MC. Join shoulder seam.

BUTTONBAND

Using 5mm (no. 6) needles and with RS facing, rejoin MC to inner end of 8 sts on left front st holder.
Work in garter st until band, when slightly stretched, fits up left front edge to beg of neck shaping, ending with a WS row. Break off yarn. Leave sts on a st holder. Sew in place. Mark positions for 7 buttons with pins, the first on ninth/tenth rows from lower edge, the last 2cm (³/₄in) below beg of neck shaping, with the remaining buttons spaced evenly between.

BUTTONHOLE BAND

Using 5mm (no. 6) needles and with WS facing, rejoin MC to inner end of 8 sts on right front st holder.
Next row: k8.
Buttonhole row 1 (RS): k3, cast off next 2 sts, knit to end.
Buttonhole row 2: k3, cast on 2 sts, k3.
Complete to match buttonband, working buttonholes to correspond with markers. Do not break off yarn.

COLLAR

Using 5mm (no. 6) needles, with RS facing and MC, knit across 8 sts of buttonhole band and 6 sts on right front safety pin, pick up and knit 15 sts up right front neck, knit across 27 sts of back neck, pick up and knit 15 sts down left front neck, knit across 6 sts on left front safety pin and 8 sts of buttonband (85 sts). Work in garter st. Cast off 3 sts at beg of next 2 rows (79 sts). Work 4 rows.

Next row: k3, (inc in next st, k3) to end (98 sts).

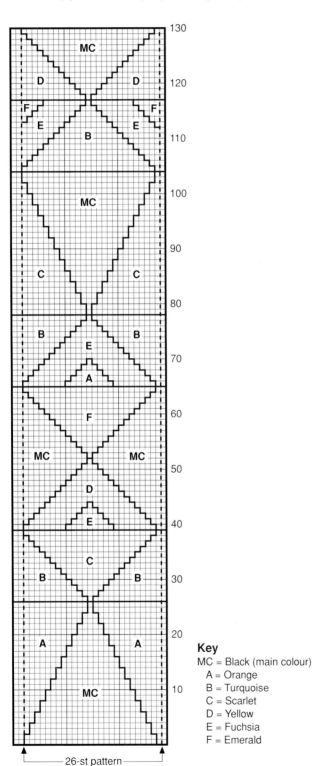

Key
MC = Black (main colour)
 A = Orange
 B = Turquoise
 C = Scarlet
 D = Yellow
 E = Fuchsia
 F = Emerald

26-st pattern

Cont in garter st until collar measures 10cm (4in). Cast off loosely.

MAKING UP

Place markers on side edges of back and fronts 29cm (11½in) from shoulder seams. Sew on sleeves between the markers. Join side and sleeve seams. Sew on buttons.

COAT

BACK

Work as back of jacket to *.
Work rows 1–38 again. **Shape shoulder.**
Work as back of jacket using C instead of MC.

LEFT FRONT

Work as left front of jacket to ***.
Work rows 117–130, then work rows 1–24 again.
Complete as left front of jacket using C instead of MC for shoulder shaping.

RIGHT FRONT

Work as right front of jacket to ****.
Change to 5½mm (no. 5) needles. Complete to match left front, ending row 25 before shaping neck.

SLEEVES

Work as jacket.

BUTTONBAND

Work as jacket, marking positions for 9 buttons.

BUTTONHOLE BAND

Work as jacket.

MAKING UP

Work as jacket.

POCKET (OPTIONAL)

Before joining the side seams, place markers for pocket positions on the back and fronts, 15cm (6in) and 30cm (12in) above the hemline for the jacket and 45cm (18in) and 60cm (24in) above the hemline for the coat.
Pocket bags: using 5½mm (no. 5) needles and with RS facing, pick up and knit 24 sts between markers on back. Beg with a purl row, work 15cm (6in) in st st, ending with a purl row. Cast off.
Pocket edgings: using 5mm (no. 6) needles, with RS facing and MC, pick up and knit 24 sts between markers on fronts. Knit 1 row. Cast off.
Join the side seams, sewing the pocket bags to wrong side of fronts. Catch down row ends of pocket edgings.

Fantasy jumper

This multicoloured floral jumper is designed for knitters who like a challenge and who are used to working with lots of colours. It is one of my personal favourites.

SIZE To fit bust 82–92cm (32–36in). Actual size: 104cm (41in) bust; 63cm (25in) long; 51cm (20in) sleeve.

MATERIALS Melinda Coss Mohair: Natural (main colour) 450gm, Candyfloss 20gm, Emerald 10gm, Black 20gm, Mauve 35gm, Royal 10gm, Yellow 25gm, Jade 10gm, Turquoise 10gm, Azure 25gm, Pink 20gm, Scarlet 20gm.

NEEDLES One pair of 4mm (no. 8) needles and one pair of 5mm (no. 6) needles. Stitch holder.

TENSION Using 5mm (no. 6) needles and measured over st st, 18 sts and 20 rows = 10cm square (4in square).

NB When working from the charts strand the yarn not in use loosely across the WS of the work to prevent puckering, weaving strands in every 2 or 3 sts to avoid long floats.
When the symbol on the charts representing a mauve bobble is reached, p1, k1, p1 into the stitch indicated (making 3 sts out of 1 st), turn, k3, turn, p3, slip the second and third sts over the first st.

BACK

Using 4mm (no. 8) needles and main colour, cast on 84 sts. Work in k1, p1 rib for 2 rows.
Change to azure and work 2 rows in rib as set.
Change to main colour and cont as set until rib measures 8cm (3¼in), inc 10 sts evenly across last row of rib (94 sts).
Change to 5mm (no. 6) needles and, working in st st throughout, begin to follow chart for back. Work straight until row 110 has been completed. Cast off loosely.

FRONT

Work as for back until row 62 has been completed then **shape neck.**
Row 63: work pattern for 29 sts and leave on a st holder.
Cast off centre 36 sts and work pattern to end. Working on this set of 29 sts, cont straight, foll chart until row 110 has been worked. Cast off loosely.

Rejoin yarn to neck edge of rem sts and cont straight, foll chart until row 110 has been worked. Cast off loosely.

SLEEVES

(Use separate chart for each sleeve.) Using 4mm (no. 8) needles and main colour, cast on 38 sts and work in rib as for back for 8cm (3¼in), inc 18 sts evenly across last row of rib (56 sts). Change to 5mm (no. 6) needles and work in st st from the appropriate chart, **at the same time** inc 1 st at each end of the fourth row and then every foll sixth row until there are 84 sts. Cont straight, foll chart until row 87 has been worked. Cast off loosely.

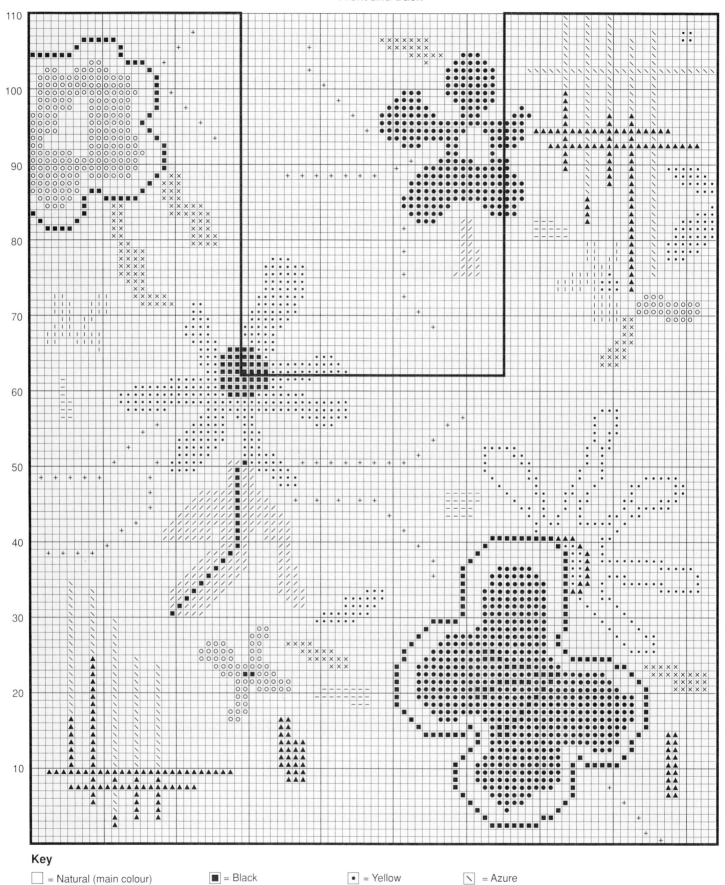

Key

☐ = Natural (main colour)	■ = Black	● = Yellow	＼ = Azure
○ = Candyfloss	+ = Mauve bobble	╱ = Jade	▲ = Pink
✕ = Emerald	I = Royal	− = Turquoise	● = Scarlet

Left Sleeve

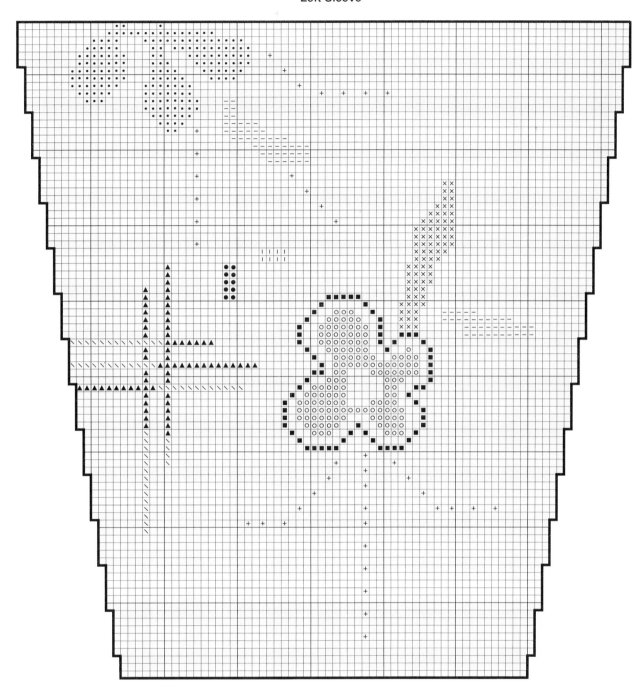

COLLAR

Using 4mm (no. 8) needles and main colour, cast on 138 sts.
Work in k1, p1 rib for 18cm (7¼in).
Change to azure and rib 2 rows.

Change to main colour and rib 2 rows. Cast off ribwise using a 5mm (no. 6) needle.

Right Sleeve

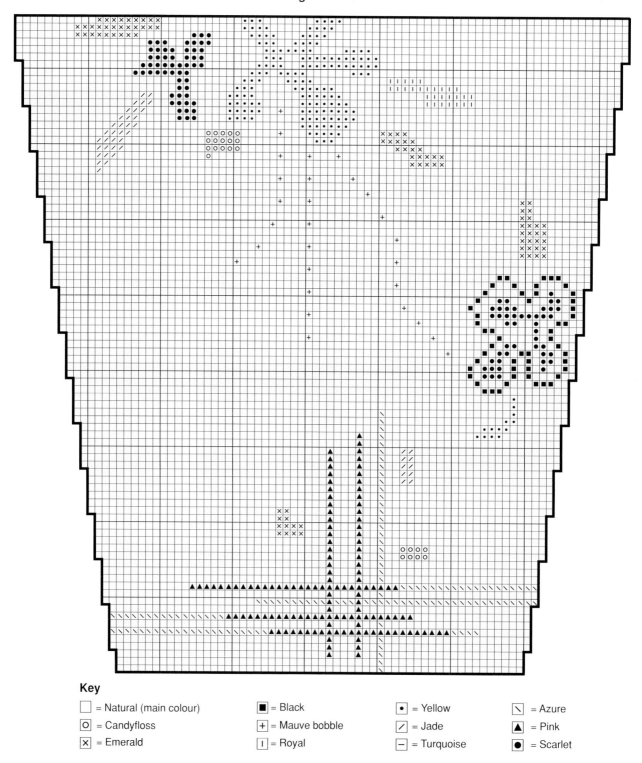

Key

☐ = Natural (main colour)	■ = Black	• = Yellow	╲ = Azure
O = Candyfloss	+ = Mauve bobble	╱ = Jade	▲ = Pink
✕ = Emerald	I = Royal	— = Turquoise	● = Scarlet

MAKING UP

Lay out the front and back and pin shoulder seams together, making sure that they match. Using a flat stitch, sew these together. Sew the collar into position, crossing the right front over the left. With centre of cast-off edges of sleeves to shoulder seams, sew sleeves carefully into position, matching patterns at front. Join side and sleeve seams.

WARM ROSE JACKET

While this jacket appears to be very complicated to knit, it is actually made up of two relatively simple motifs produced in an assortment of colourways. To make life easy for yourself, sort the yarns into groups before you begin. You will find that the end result is well worth the effort involved.

SIZE To fit bust 86–102cm (34–40in). Actual size: 132.5cm (52¼in) bust; 81.5cm (32in) long; 52.5cm (20¾in) sleeve seam.

MATERIALS Melinda Coss Mohair: Smoke (main colour A) 550gm, Coral Rose 50gm, Apple 45gm, Red, Peach, Mustard, 25gm of each, Crimson, Yellow, Pinky Red, Pale May, Ecru, Lemon, Fuchsia, Bright Pink, Pale Pink, Olive, 20gm of each. 6 pearl buttons.

NEEDLES One pair 4½mm (no. 7) needles and one pair 5½mm (no. 5) needles. Row counter.

TENSION Using 5½mm (no. 5) needles and measured over st st, 16 sts and 20 rows = 10cm (4in square).

BACK

Using 4½mm (no. 7) needles and A, cast on 92 sts and work in single rib for 6.5cm (2½in), inc 10 sts evenly across last row of rib (102 sts).

Change to 5½mm (no. 5) needles and put row counter at nil. Working in st st throughout, place charts as follows.

Row 5: k6A, work across 46 sts of chart 1 in colourway 1, k50A to end. This sets your position for chart 1, work 28 rows until complete. **At the same time**, when counter reads row 11 (you are on your seventh row of chart 1), k6A, work across 46 sts of chart 1, k10A, knit across first row of chart 2 in colourway 2, k6A to end.

Cont working from these two charts in colourways as set until counter reads row 41: k12A, knit across first row of chart 2 in colourway 1, k56A to end. Keeping chart 2 in this position work until counter reads row 47: k12A, knit across row 7 of chart 2, k4A, knit across 46 sts (row 1) of chart 1, using colourway 2, k6A to end.

Keeping both charts in position as set, work until they are complete, then continue in A until row counter reads row 81: k10A, knit across first row of chart 1 using colourway 1, k46A, to end. Keeping chart in this position work one more row.

Row 83: k10A, knit across third row of chart 1, k3A, knit across first row (34 sts) of chart 2 using colourway 1. Complete both these charts in positions and colourways as set. **At the same time** when counter reads row 107, **shape armholes.**

Cast off 7 sts at beg of this row and the next row. Work straight to row 113: k1A, work across first row of chart 2 in colourway 2, k51A to end. Follow chart to row 121: k1, work across row 9 of chart 2, k4A, knit across 46 sts of chart 1 in colourway 2, k3A to end.

Keep charts in position as set until they are complete. Continue in A only to row 151. **Shape shoulders.**

Cast off 9 sts at beg of the next 2 rows, then cast off 8 sts at beg of the 4 foll rows. Cast off remaining sts.

RIGHT FRONT

Using 4½mm (no. 7) needles and A, cast on 46 sts and work in single rib for 6.5cm (2½in), inc 5 sts evenly across last row of rib (51 sts).

Change to 5½mm (no. 5) needles and put row counter at nil.

Cont in st st in A only until counter reads row 7: k2A, knit across first row of chart 1 in colourway 2, k3 to end.

Work the 28 rows of chart in colourway and position as set, then cont in A only to row 41: k7A, knit across first row of chart 2 in colourway 1, k10A to end.

Keeping chart and colourway in position as set, work 30 rows until it is complete then cont in A to row 81: k4A, knit across first row of chart 1 using colourway 1, k1A. Cont in A only to row 108. **Shape armhole.**

Cast off 8 sts at beg of this row. Work 3 more rows.

Row 112: **shape neck.**

Purl in A to last 2 sts, p2tog. Dec 1 st at neck edge on the foll 12 alt rows. **At the same time** when counter reads row 115: k6A, knit across first row of chart 2 in colourway 2, k1A to end. Cont working chart in this position but leave out the top leaf. When chart is complete, cont in A only to row 152. **Shape shoulder.**

Cast off 9 sts at beg of this row, 8 sts at beg of the foll 2 alt rows. Work 1 row, cast off remaining 5 sts.

LEFT FRONT

Work as for right front but in reverse (i.e. work row 1 in purl and read charts as purl row 1, still reading from right to left, and knit row 2, reading from left to right, etc. Also use colourway 2 when colourway 1 is quoted, and vice versa).

RIGHT SLEEVE

Using 5½mm (no. 5) needles and A, cast on 51 sts. Work in single rib for 16.5cm (6½in). Place row counter at nil. Begin working in st st, inc 1 st at each end of the fourth row and every foll third row until you have 59 sts. Then increase 1 st each end of every foll fourth row until you have 85 sts. Work 7 rows straight. **At the same time** place charts as follows.

Row 3: k15A, knit across first row of chart 2 in colourway 1, k2A to end. Work in this position until chart is complete.

Row 41: k15A, knit across first row of chart 1 in colourway 1, k10A to end.

Work in this position until chart is complete, then continue in A only until sleeve is complete. Cast off loosely.

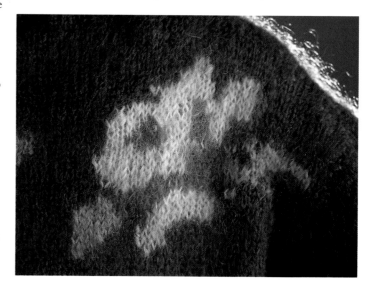

LEFT SLEEVE

Work as for right sleeve but use colourway 2 on both charts.

BUTTONBAND AND LEFT COLLAR

Using 4½mm (no. 7) needles and A, cast on 18 sts and work in single rib until band fits up front edge to beg of front shaping when slightly stretched.
Next row (RS): rib 2, inc 2 sts in next st, rib to end.
Next 3 rows, rib to end. Repeat last 4 rows 12 times more.
Next row: rib 2, inc 2, rib to end (46 sts).
Work straight until band fits up front edge to centre back neck, when slightly stretched. Cast off in rib.
Using pins, mark 6 button positions, the first one 3cm (1¼in) from cast-on edge, the last one 2cm (¾in) from beg of collar shaping and the remainder evenly spaced in between.

BUTTONHOLE BAND AND RIGHT COLLAR

Work as for buttonband, reversing the shapings by reading RS row for WS row and working buttonholes to correspond with pins as follows.
Buttonhole row (RS): rib 7, cast off 3, rib to end.
On return row cast on 3 sts over those previously cast off.

MAKING UP

Join shoulder seams, set in sleeves, then join side and sleeve seams. Sew buttonbands and collars into position and join cast-off edges of collar invisibly at centre back neck.

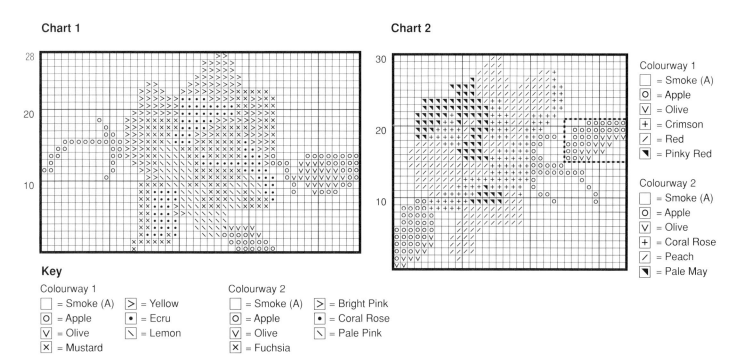

Chart 1

Chart 2

Key

Colourway 1

☐ = Smoke (A) | > = Yellow
O = Apple | • = Ecru
V = Olive | \ = Lemon
X = Mustard

Colourway 2

☐ = Smoke (A) | > = Bright Pink
O = Apple | • = Coral Rose
V = Olive | \ = Pale Pink
X = Fuchsia

Colourway 1

☐ = Smoke (A)
O = Apple
V = Olive
+ = Crimson
/ = Red
◣ = Pinky Red

Colourway 2

☐ = Smoke (A)
O = Apple
V = Olive
+ = Coral Rose
/ = Peach
◣ = Pale May

PATCHWORK JACKET

This design was based on an American patchwork quilt. Worked using the intarsia method (see p. 8), it has no chart to follow and the soft pastel colours are both pretty and flattering.

SIZE To fit bust 86–102cm (34–40in). Actual size: 129cm (50³/4in) bust; 78.5cm (31in) long; 42cm (16¹/2in) sleeve seam.

MATERIALS Melinda Coss Mohair: Black (A) 170gm, Cream (B) 270gm, Mid Blue (C) 35gm, Pink (D) 70gm, Silver (E) 170gm. 8 buttons.

NEEDLES One pair of 5¹/2mm (no. 5) needles and one pair of 4¹/2mm (no. 7) needles. Stitch holder.

TENSION Using 5¹/2mm (no. 5) needles and measured over st st, 16 sts and 20 rows = 10cm square (4in square).

BACK

Using 4¹/2mm (no. 7) needles and A, cast on 100 sts and work in k1, p1 rib for 3.5cm (1¹/2in).

Change to 5¹/2mm (no. 5) needles. Joining in and cutting off colours as required and working in st st throughout, work in pattern as follows.

Row 1 (RS): using A, knit to end.
Row 2: purl 1A, (23B, 2A, 5B, 1C, 5B, 1D, 5B, 1A, 5B, 2A) to end, ending last rep 1A.
Row 3: 1A, (4B, 2A, 4B, 3D, 4B, 2C, 4B, 2A, 23E, 2A) to end, ending last rep 1A.
Row 4: 1A, (23E, 2A, 3B, 3C, 3B, 5D, 3B, 3A, 3B, 2A) to end, ending last rep 1A.
Row 5: 1A, (2B, 4A, 2B, 7D, 2B, 4C, 2B, 2A, 23B, 2A) to end, ending last rep 1A.
Row 6: 1A, (23B, 2A, 1B, 5C, 1B, 2E, 5D, 2E, 1B, 5A, 1B, 2A) to end, ending last rep 1A.
Row 7: 7A, (4E, 3D, 4E, 6C, 2A, 23B, 8A) to end, ending last rep 1A.
Row 8: 1A, (23B, 2A, 5B, 6E, 1D, 6E, 5B, 2A) to end, ending last rep 1A.
Row 9: 1A, (4B, 7E, 1B, 7E, 4B, 2A, 23E, 2A) to end, ending last rep 1A.
Row 10: 1A, (23E, 2A, 3B, 1D, 6E, 3B, 6E, 1D, 3B, 2A) to end, ending last rep 1A.
Row 11: 1A, (2B, 3D, 4E, 5B, 4E, 3D, 2B, 2A, 23B, 2A) to end, ending last rep 1A.
Row 12: 1A, (23B, 2A, 1B, 5D, 2E, 7B, 2E, 5D, 1B, 2A) to end, ending last rep 1A.

Row 13: 1A, (7D, 9B, 7D, 2A, 23B, 2A) to end, ending last rep 1A.
Row 14: as row 12.
Row 15: 1A, (2B, 3D, 4E, 5B, 4E, 3D, 2B, 2A, 23E, 2A) to end, ending last rep 1A.
Row 16: as row 10.
Row 17: 1A, (4B, 7E, 1B, 7E, 4B, 2A, 23B, 2A) to end, ending last rep 1A.
Row 18: as row 8.
Row 19: 1A, (6C, 4E, 3D, 4E, 8A, 23B, 2A) to end, ending last rep 1A.
Row 20: 1A, (23B, 2A, 1B, 5A, 1B, 2E, 5D, 2E, 1B, 5C, 1B, 2A) to end, ending last rep 1A.
Row 21: 1A, (2B, 4C, 2B, 7D, 2B, 4A, 2B, 2A, 23E, 2A) to end, ending last rep 1A.
Row 22: 1A, (23E, 2A, 3B, 3A, 3B, 5D, 3B, 3C, 3B, 2A) to end, ending last rep 1A.
Row 23: 1A, (4B, 2C, 4B, 3D, 4B, 2A, 4B, 2A, 23B, 2A) to end, ending last rep 1A.
Row 24: 1A, (23B, 2A, 5B, 1A, 5B, 1D, 5B, 1C, 5B, 2A) to end, ending last rep 1A.
Rows 25 and 26: using A, work to end.
Row 27: as row 24.
Row 28: 1A, (4B, 2C, 4B, 3D, 4B, 2A, 4B, 2A, 23E, 2A) to end, ending last rep 1A.
Row 29: as row 22.
Row 30: 1A, (2B, 4C, 2B, 7D, 2B, 4A, 2B, 2A, 23B, 2A) to end, ending last rep 1A.
Row 31: as row 20.
Row 32: as row 19.
Rows 33–38: as rows 8–13.
Row 39: as row 12.
Row 40: as row 15.
Row 41: as row 10.
Row 42: as row 17.
Rows 43–45: as rows 8–6 in that order.
Row 46: 1A, (2B, 4A, 2B, 7D, 2B, 4C, 2B, 2A, 23E, 2A) to end, ending last rep 1A.
Row 47: as row 4.
Row 48: 1A, (4B, 2A, 4B, 3D, 4B, 2C, 4B, 2A, 23B, 2A) to end, ending last rep 1A.
Row 49: as row 2.
Row 50: using A, work to end.
These 50 rows form the pattern. Rep them twice more. **Then shape shoulder.**
Next row: using A, cast off 34, cut off yarn and sl next 32 sts (including st on right-hand needle) on to a holder, join in yarn to next st, cast off rem 34 sts.

LEFT FRONT

*Using 4½mm (no. 7) needles and A, cast on 50 sts and work in k1, p1 rib for 3.5cm (1½in).

Change to 5½mm (no. 5) needles. Joining in and cutting off colours as required and working in st st throughout, work in pattern as follows.

Row 1 (RS): using A, work to end.
Row 2: 1A, 23B, 2A, 5B, 1C, 5B, 1D, 5B, 1A, 5B, 1A.
Row 3: 1A, 4B, 2A, 4B, 3D, 4B, 2C, 4B, 2A, 23E, 1A.
Row 4: 1A, 23E, 2A, 3B, 3C, 3B, 5D, 3B, 3A, 3B, 1A.

These 4 rows place the pattern. Keeping pattern correct throughout, work straight until front measures approx 72.5cm (28½in) from cast-on edge, ending pattern at row 38.* **Shape neck.**

Next row: pattern 42, turn and leave rem 8 sts on a holder.
Cast off 2 sts at beg of next and every foll alt row until 34 sts rem. Work 4 rows straight (for right front read '3 rows' here), so ending pattern at row 50. Cast off.

RIGHT FRONT

Work as given for left front from * to *. **Shape neck.**

Next row: cut off yarn, sl first 8 sts on to a holder, join in yarn to next st and pattern to end of row (42 sts). Work 1 row.
Complete as given for first side from ** to **, noting the bracketed exception.

SLEEVES

(Both alike.) Using 4½mm (no. 7) needles and A, cast on 45 sts.
Rib row 1 (RS): k1, (p1, k1) to end.
Rib row 2: p1, (k1, p1) to end.
Rep these 2 rows for 4cm (1½in), ending rib at row 2.
Change to 5½mm (no. 5) needles. Joining in and cutting off colours as required and working in st st throughout, work in pattern as follows.

Row 1: using A, inc in first st, work to within last st, inc in last st (47 sts).
Row 2: 10B, 2A, 5B, 1C, 5B, 1D, 5B, 1A, 5B, 2A, 10B.
Row 3: 10E, 2A, 4B, 2A, 4B, 3D, 4B, 2C, 4B, 2A, 10E.
Row 4: using E, inc in first st, 9E, 2A, 3B, 3C, 3B, 5D, 3B, 3A, 3B, 2A, 9E, with E, inc in last st (49 sts).

These 4 rows place the pattern. Taking extra sts into pattern, inc one st each end of every foll third row until there are 71 sts, then each end of every foll fourth row until there are 77 sts.
Taking extra sts into B only, inc 1 st each end of every foll fourth row until there are 89 sts.
Work 3 rows straight, so ending pattern at row 26. Cast off.

NECKBAND

Join shoulder seams. With RS facing and using a 4½mm (no. 7) needle and A, knit across right front neck sts from holder, knit up 20 sts from right front neck, knit across back neck sts from holder, inc 1 st at centre, knit up 20 sts from left front neck, then knit across left front neck sts from holder (89 sts). Work in rib as given for cuff for 3.5cm (1½in). Cast off in rib.

BUTTONBAND

Using 4½mm (no. 7) needles and A, cast on 9 sts and work in rib as given for cuff until band, slightly stretched, fits up left front edge to top of neckband. Cast off in rib.
Mark 8 button positions, the first 3cm (1¼in) from cast-on edge, the last 1.5cm (¾in) from cast-off edge and the remainder evenly spaced between.

BUTTONHOLE BAND

Work to match buttonband, making buttonholes to correspond with markers as follows.
Buttonhole row 1 (RS): rib 4, cast off 2, rib to end.
Buttonhole row 2: rib, casting on 2 sts over those cast off.

MAKING UP

Do not press.
Sew sleeves to main part, matching centre of each sleeve top to shoulder seam, then join side and sleeve seams. Sew front bands in position. Sew on buttons.

ARGYLL COAT

This full-length raglan coat is a new interpretation of an old theme. The Argyll pattern is timeless, so why not add bold and beautiful colours and wear it to brighten up the gloomiest day?

SIZE To fit bust 86–102cm (34–40in). Actual size: 139.5cm (55in) bust; 101cm (40in) long; 26.5cm (10½in) sleeve seam.

MATERIALS Melinda Coss Mohair: Black (A) 310gm, Orange (B) 75gm, Emerald (C) 100gm, Scarlet (D) 75gm, Yellow (E) 120gm, Turquoise (F) 75gm, Fuchsia (G) 75gm, Royal (H) 75gm, Purple (J) 100gm. 4 large square buttons.

NEEDLES One pair of 5mm (no. 6) needles and one pair of 5½mm (no. 5) needles.

TENSION Using 5½mm (no. 5) needles and measured over st st, 16 sts and 21 rows = 10cm square (4in square).

Sleeves

Key

⬤ = Black (A)
B = Orange
C = Emerald
D = Scarlet
E = Yellow
F = Turquoise
G = Fuchsia
H = Royal
J = Purple

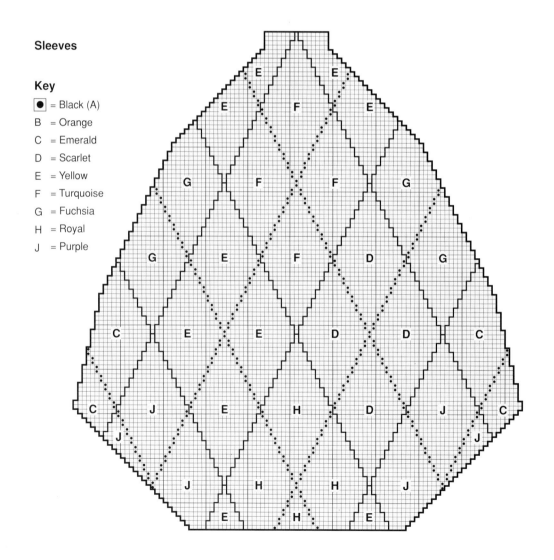

BACK

Using 5mm (no. 6) needles and A, cast on 103 sts. *Working in st st throughout, work straight for 8cm (3in), ending on a WS row. Change to 5½mm (no. 5) needles and work in pattern from chart until row 120 has been completed.* **Shape raglan.**
Keeping chart correct throughout, dec 1 st each end of next and every foll alt row until 21 sts remain. Work 3 rows straight so chart is complete, then cast off.

LEFT FRONT

Using 5mm (no. 5) needles and A, cast on 52 sts. Work as given for back from * to *. **Shape raglan.**
Keeping chart correct throughout, dec 1 st at beg (for right front read 'end' here) of next and every foll alt row until 48 sts rem. Work 1 row, so ending row 128 of chart. **Shape front edge.**
Cont to dec 1 st at raglan edge on next and every foll alt row as before, **at the same time** dec 1 st at front edge on next and every foll eighth row until 6 sts rem, so ending row 193 of chart. Dec 1 st at raglan edge only on every foll alt row until 2 sts rem. Work 3 rows straight, so completing chart. Cast off.

RIGHT FRONT

Work as given for left front, noting the bracketed exception.

SLEEVES

(Both alike.) Using 5mm (no. 6) needles and A, cast on 48 sts and knit 4 rows. Now work in k6, p6 rib until cuff measures 12.5cm (5in), inc 3 sts evenly across last row of rib (51 sts).
Change to 5½mm (no. 5) needles and work in st st throughout from chart. Keeping chart correct, inc 1 st each end of every row until you have 105 sts. Work 1 row, so ending row 29 of chart. **Shape raglan.**
Dec 1 st each end of next and every foll fourth row until 91 sts rem. Then dec 1 st each end of every alt row 17 times (57 sts), then each end of every row until 15 sts rem. Work 3 rows straight, so completing chart. Cast off.

BUTTON BORDER AND COLLAR

Join raglan and side seams. Make a hem by folding the first 4cm (1½in) at lower edge of coat to WS and sewing into position.
Using 5mm (no. 6) needles and A, cast on 30 sts.
Rib row 1: k6 (p6, k6) twice.
Rib row 2: p6 (k6, p6) twice.
Repeat these two rows until border, slightly stretched, fits up left front edge to centre back neck. Cast off in rib.
Sew border in position. Mark 4 button positions, the first 16cm (6¼in) from cast-on edge, the last level with start of front shaping, and the rest evenly spaced in between.

BUTTONHOLE BORDER AND COLLAR

Work to match button border and collar, making buttonholes to correspond with markers as follows.
Buttonhole row 1 (RS): rib 14, cast off 2, rib to end.
Buttonhole row 2: rib, casting on 2 sts over those cast off.

MAKING UP

Do not press. Join cast-off edges of collar at centre back neck. Join sleeve seams. Sew on buttons.

Back and Fronts

Key

- ● = Black (A)
- B = Orange
- C = Emerald
- D = Scarlet
- E = Yellow
- F = Turquoise
- G = Fuchsia
- H = Royal
- J = Purple

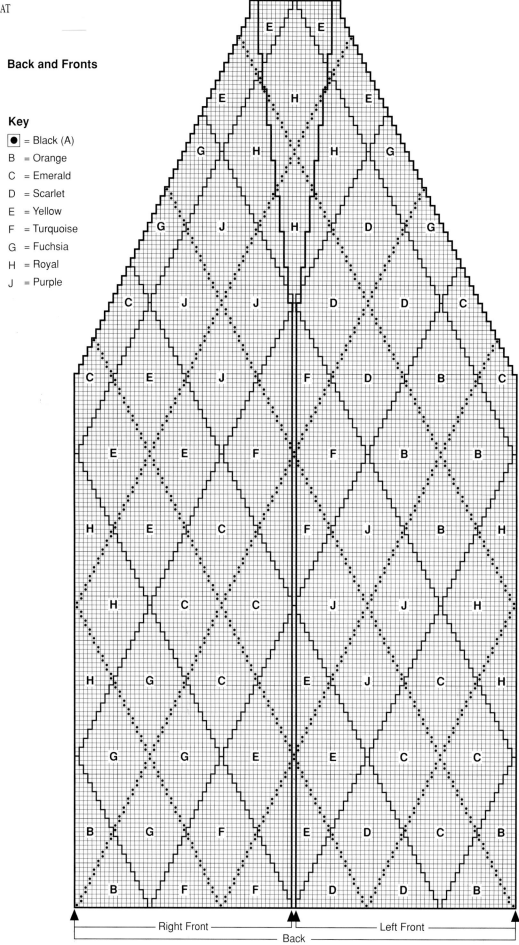

Right Front — Back — Left Front

PRISCILLA COAT

This coat is one for those who enjoy multi-coloured work. It is based on one of my own cats, Priscilla, who, since she became a star, has taken to demanding chicken liver instead of the statutory Whiskas enjoyed by the rest of the family. Worked using the intarsia method (see p. 8), its front is curved and based on the same shape as 'Exclusively Yours' (see p. 34).

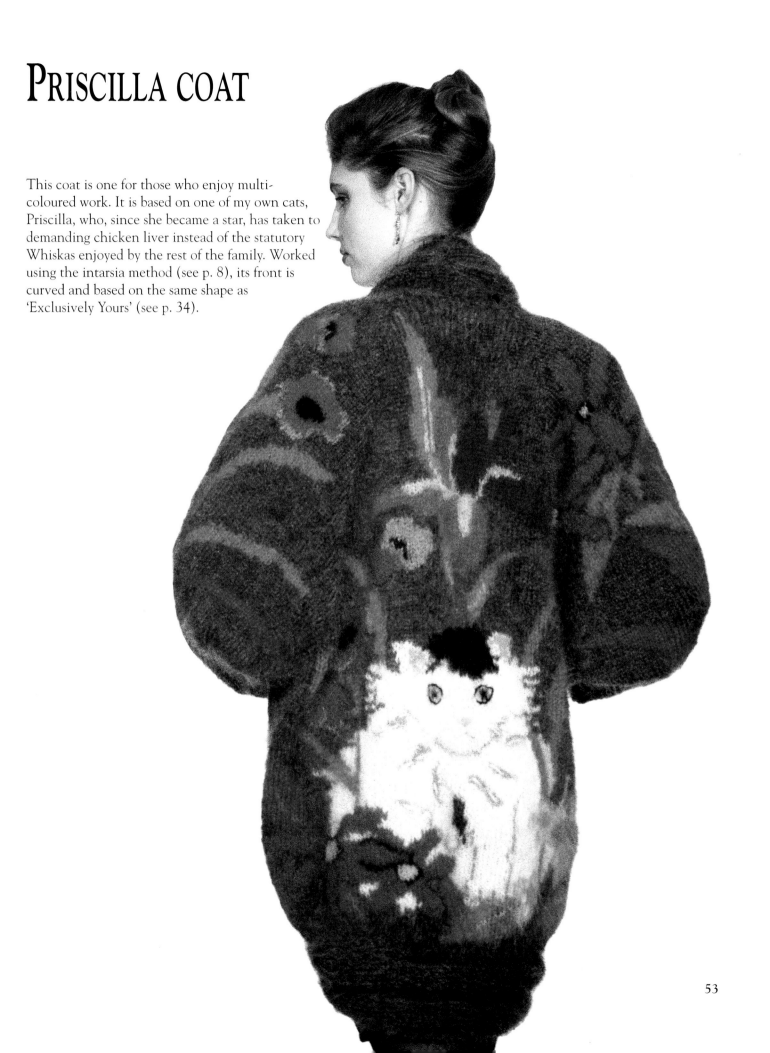

SIZE To fit bust 92–112cm (36–44in). Actual size: 150cm (59in) bust; 94cm (37in) long.

MATERIALS Melinda Coss Mohair: Charcoal 525gm, Emerald 100gm, Jade, Fuchsia and White, 50gm of each, Mid Blue, Lemon, Gold, Purple, Orange, Black, Coral, Scarlet, Silver and Pink, less than 25gm of each.

NEEDLES One pair of 5½mm (no. 5) needles.

TENSION Using 5½mm (no. 5) needles and measured over st st, 16 sts and 16 rows = 10cm square (4in square).

BACK

Using 5½mm (no. 5) needles and main colour, cast on 112 sts.
Beginning with a knit row, follow chart for back in st st to beg of raglan shaping.
Cast off 2 sts at beg of the next 2 rows, then dec 1 st at each end of every alt row until chart is complete. Cast off remaining 18 sts.

RIGHT FRONT

Using 5½mm (no. 5) needles and main colour, cast on 8 sts.
Begin following the chart in st st, casting on 7 sts at end of the second row.
Work 2 rows, casting on 5 sts at end of the second row and the foll alt row.
Knit 1 row, purl 1 row, cast on 3 sts. Knit 1 row, purl 1 row, cast on 2 sts. Knit 1 row, purl back, inc once in the last st. Cont to inc 1 st at shaped edge on every row until you have 49 sts. Then inc 1 st at every alt row until you have 59 sts.
Cont straight, without further shaping, until 71 rows have been completed from beg of work. Then **shape armholes.**
Next row (WS): cast off 2 sts at beg of row.
Cast off 1 st at armhole edge on the next 8 alt rows (49 sts).
Work 1 row. Cont to dec 1 st at armhole edge on every alt row.
Shape neck.
Cast off 1 st at neck edge on next row and the 11 following sixth rows. Work straight at neck edge for 5 rows, while cont to shape sleeve edge until you have 1 st. Fasten off.

LEFT FRONT

Work as for right front, but read left front chart and reverse shapings.

SLEEVES

(Both alike.) Using 5½mm (no. 5) needles and main colour, cast on 48 sts. Begin following the appropriate chart, working the first 4 rows in garter stitch.
Then work in k6, p6 rib for 22 rows, inc 5 sts evenly across last row of rib (53 sts).
Cont following chart, working in st st and inc 1 st at each end of every row until you have 109 sts.
Work 3 rows without shaping, then dec 1 st at each end of the next row and the 6 following fourth rows, then every alt row 27

times (41 sts), then at each end of every row until you have 11 sts. Cast off.

COLLAR

(Knitted in one piece.) Using 5½mm (no. 5) needles, cast on 30 sts.
Row 1: k6, p6, k6, p6, k6.
Row 2: p6, k6, p6, k6, p6.
Repeat these 2 rows until the border fits all around the outer edge of the coat, beginning and ending at the centre-back neck. Cast off.

MAKING UP

Join raglan seams of back and sleeves, then join each front raglan to sleeves. Join side and sleeve seams using invisible seams throughout.

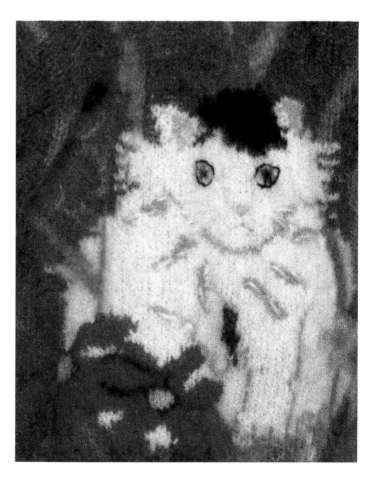

Back

Key

A = Charcoal (main colour)
M = Mid Blue
P = Purple
Y = Gold
X = Black
G = Emerald
J = Jade
C = Coral
R = Scarlet
⊘ = Silver
S = Pink
L = Lemon
△ = Orange
F = Fuchsia
O = White

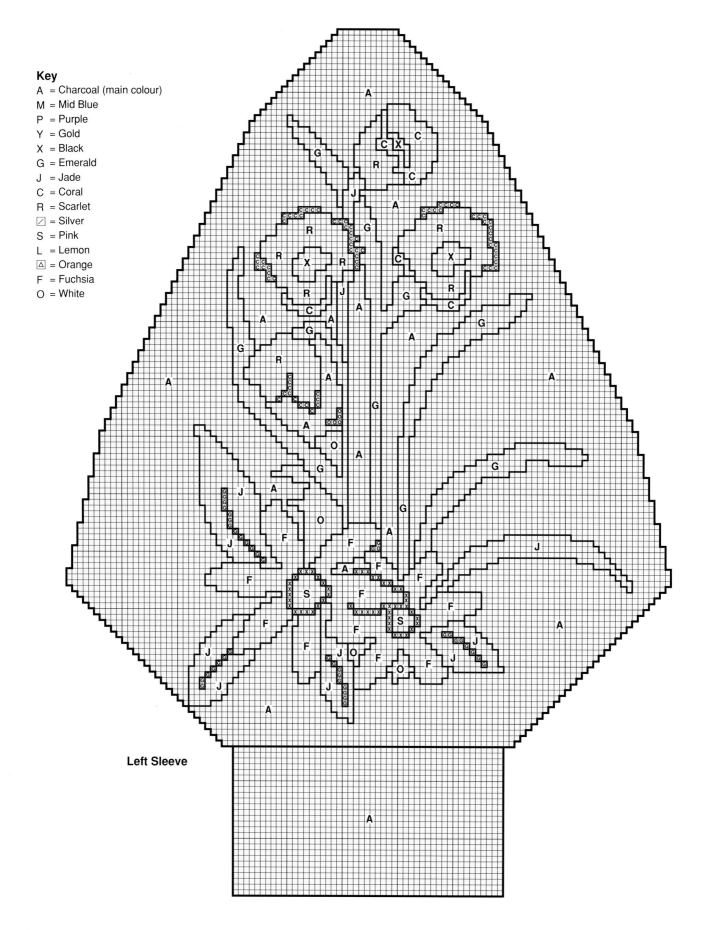

Key

A = Charcoal (main colour)
M = Mid Blue
P = Purple
Y = Gold
X = Black
G = Emerald
J = Jade
C = Coral
R = Scarlet
◻ = Silver
S = Pink
L = Lemon
△ = Orange
F = Fuchsia
O = White

Left Sleeve

56

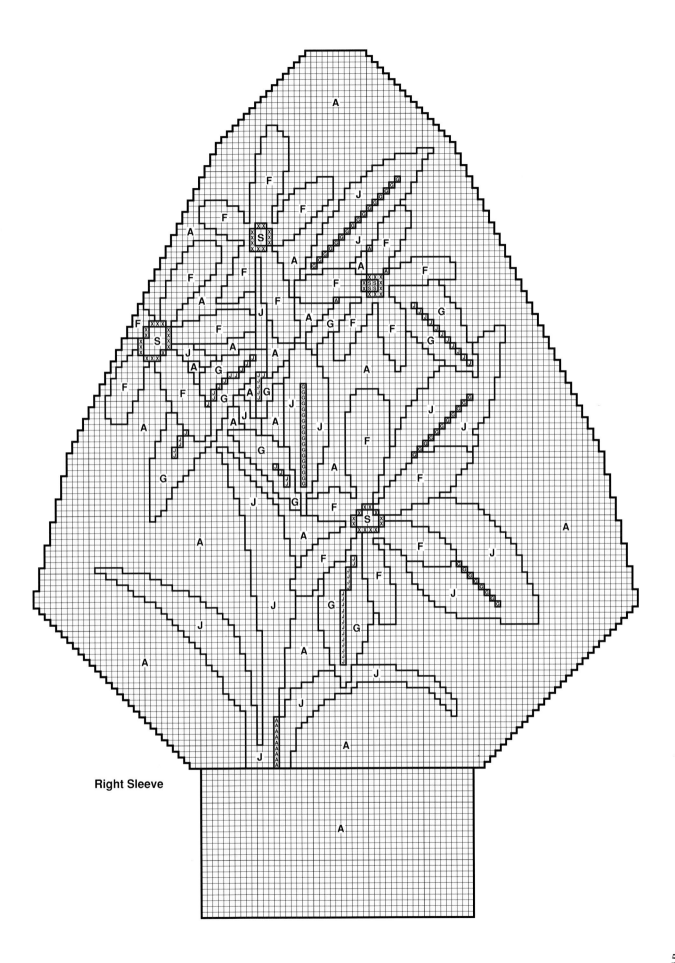

Right Sleeve

Right Front

Left Front

Key

A = Charcoal (main colour)
M = Mid Blue
P = Purple
Y = Gold
X = Black
G = Emerald
J = Jade
C = Coral
R = Scarlet
◿ = Silver
S = Pink
L = Lemon
◿ = Orange
F = Fuchsia
O = White

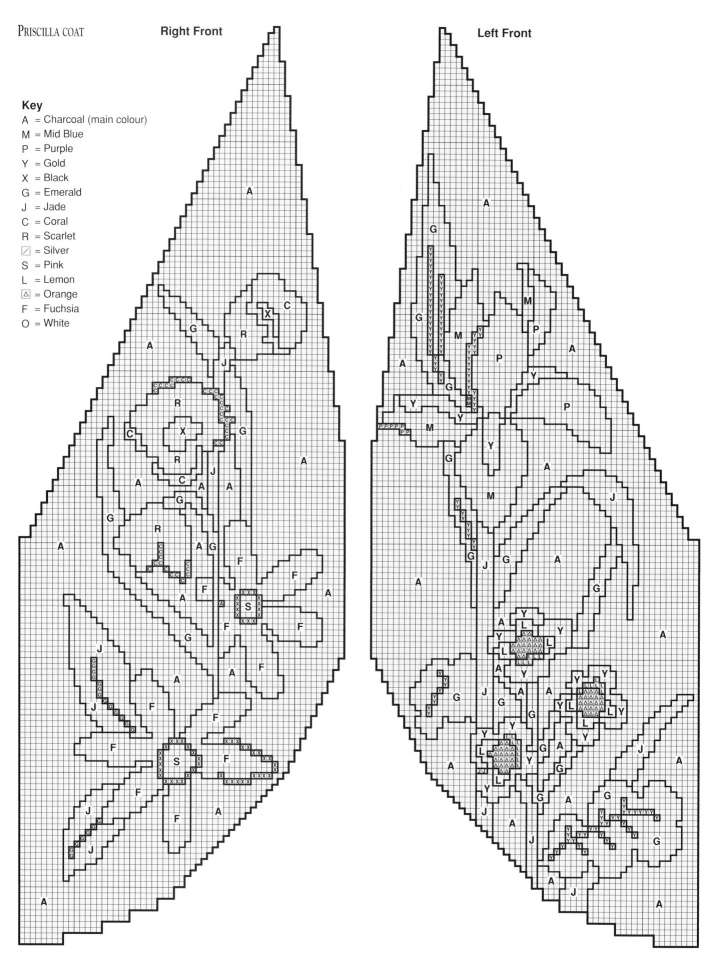

PIERROT JUMPER

This smart jumper has a Sixties flavour and can be dressed up or down and knitted in colours that match your wardrobe. It is a simple crew-necked dropped-sleeve shape.

SIZE To fit bust 91–107cm (36–40in). Actual size: 120cm (47in) bust; 63cm (25in) long; 43½cm (17in) sleeve.

MATERIALS Melinda Coss Mohair: Black (A) 360gm, Yellow (Y), Royal (B), Turquoise (T), Fuchsia (F), Emerald (G), 40gm of each.

NEEDLES One pair of 4½mm (no. 7) needles and one pair of 5½mm (no. 5) needles. Stitch holder.

TENSION Using 5½mm (no. 5) needles and measured over st st, 16 sts and 21 rows = 10cm square (4in square).

NB When knitting the back, work diamond chart on *left* side in order to match up pattern when sewing up.

FRONT

Using 4½mm (no. 7) needles and black, cast on 70 sts. Work in k1, p1 rib for 8cm (3in). Inc 26 sts evenly across last row of rib (96 sts). Change to 5½mm (no. 5) needles and begin following chart, beg with a knit row and working in st st throughout.* Place chart as follows.
Row 1: k6A, k2Y, k13A, k2T, k73A.
Row 2: p72A, p4T, p11A, p4Y, p5A.
These 2 rows set your pattern. Work straight until 92 rows of chart have been completed, ending on WS row. **Shape neck.**
Pattern 34 sts, turn, leave rem sts on a st holder and work first side of neck. Cast off 1 st at the beg of the next row and at neck edge every foll row 7 times. Cast off remaining 28 sts.
Place centre 28 sts on a st holder and rejoin yarn to remaining sts. Work second side of neck to match first side.

BACK

Work as for front to *. Work straight until chart is complete, then cast off all sts.

LEFT SLEEVE

Using 4½mm (no. 7) needles and black, cast on 36 sts. Work in k1, p1 rib for 8cm (3in), increasing 20 sts evenly across last row of rib (56 sts).
Change to 5½mm (no. 5) needles.** Begin following chart for sleeve, starting with a knit row and working in st st throughout.

At the same time, inc 1 st each end of every third row until you have 82 sts. Cont straight until sleeve chart has been completed. Cast off all sts loosely.

RIGHT SLEEVE
Work as for left sleeve to **. Cont working with black, increasing as for left sleeve, then work 26 rows straight in st st. Cast off all sts loosely.
Join left shoulder seam.

NECKBAND
Using 4¹/₂mm (no. 7) needles and black, pick up and knit 7 sts down right neck edge, 28 sts across centre front, 7 sts up left neck edge, 40 sts across back neck (82 sts). Work 9 rows in k1, p1 rib. Cast off loosely in rib.

MAKING UP
Join right shoulder and neckband seam. Turn neckband inwards and slipstitch cast-off edge on to pick-up edge. Join sleeves to body, join side and sleeve seams.

Front and Back

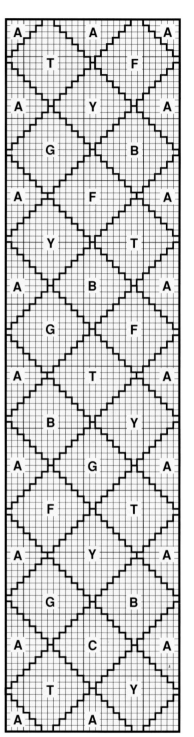

Sleeve

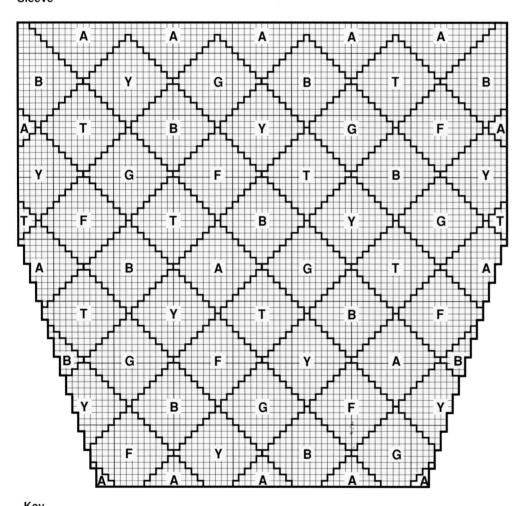

Key
A = Black   Y = Yellow   B = Royal   T = Turquoise   F = Fuchsia   G = Emerald

ARIZONA JACKET

I asked colleague author/designer Sylvie Soudan to come up with a pattern and she produced this wonderful fairisle jacket (see p. 9 for fairisle). It has been much admired in the studio, and I could not resist making one up for myself.

SIZE To fit bust 91–107cm (36–42in). Actual size: 146cm (47in) bust; 75cm (29$\frac{1}{2}$in) long; 44·5cm (17$\frac{1}{2}$in) sleeve.

MATERIALS Melinda Coss Mohair: Petrol (A) 475gm, Red 75gm, Gingy 50gm, Mustard 100gm. 4 buttons.

NEEDLES One pair of 5mm (no. 6) needles, one pair of 5$\frac{1}{2}$mm (no. 5) needles and one pair of 6mm (no. 4) needles.

TENSION Using 5$\frac{1}{2}$mm (no. 5) needles and measured over st st, 15 sts and 20 rows = 10cm square (4in square).

NB Work charts 1 and 2 with 6mm (no. 4) needles in st st. Work plain areas in A and chart 3 with 5$\frac{1}{2}$mm (no. 5) needles. When working from chart, strand yarn not in use loosely across back of work. Use separate balls of yarn for / on chart 1 (i.e. do not strand yarn across back).

BACK

Using 5mm (no. 6) needles and A, cast on 120 sts. Work 10cm (4in) in k2, p2 rib. (See note above and cont to work throughout in st st.)
Starting with a knit row, work 2 rows in A, 20 rows from chart 1, 24 rows in A, 10 rows chart 2, 12 rows A, 10 rows chart 3, 2 rows A, 20 rows chart 1, 2 rows A, 10 rows chart 2, 2 rows A. Cast off loosely.

LEFT FRONT

Using 5mm (no. 6) needles and A, cast on 50 sts. Work 10cm (4in) in k2, p2 rib. (See note above and cont to work throughout in st st.) Starting with a knit row, work 2 rows in A, 20 rows from chart 1 (beg and ending left front as indicated on chart), 24 rows A,

10 rows chart 2 (beg with 1A, repeat 24-st pattern twice, ending 1 st A).

Work 12 rows A, 10 rows chart 3 (beg with 1 st A, rep 24-st pattern twice, ending 1 st A.) Work 2 rows A. ** **Shape neck.** Cont working as follows but **at the same time** dec 1 st at the **end** of the next row and every foll fourth row until there are 40 sts. Work 20 rows chart 1, 2 rows A, 10 rows chart 2 (begin as indicated on chart), 2 rows A. Cast off loosely.

RIGHT FRONT

Work as for left front to **. **Shape neck.**
Cont working as follows but **at the same time** dec 1 st at the **beg** of the next row and every foll fourth row until there are 40 sts. Work 20 rows chart 1 (beg as indicated on chart), 2 rows A, 10 rows chart 2 (beg as indicated on chart), 2 rows A. Cast off loosely.

SLEEVES

(Both alike.) Using 5mm (no. 6) needles and A, cast on 50 sts and work 10cm (4in) in k2, p2 rib. (See note and cont to work throughout in st st.) Beginning with a knit row, work in pattern as follows. **At the same time** inc 1 st each end of every alt row until you have 110 sts.
Work 2 rows A, 20 rows chart 2, i.e. work 10 rows of chart twice (beg k1 mustard, rep pattern twice, k1A), working increases into check pattern at sides.
Work 24 rows A, 10 rows chart 2, 12 rows A. Cast off loosely. Join shoulder seams, matching pattern.

BUTTONBAND

Using 5¹/₂mm (no. 5) needles and gingy, cast on 13 sts. Work in k1, p1 rib until band fits to beg of neck shaping when slightly stretched.
Next row: rib 2, inc 2 sts into next st, keeping rib pattern correct, rib to end.
Rib 7 rows. Repeat last 8 rows until you have 25 sts. Work straight in rib until band fits up around neck to centre back. Cast off.
Sew into position and place markers for 4 buttons, the first 2cm (³/₄in) from cast-on edge and the last 1cm (¹/₃in) below the beginning of the neck shaping.

BUTTONHOLE BAND

Work as for buttonband, but at the same time work buttonholes to correspond with markers as follows:
Row 1: rib 5, cast off 3; rib 5.
Row 2: rib 5, cast on 3, rib 5.

MAKING UP

- Place centre of cast-off sleeve top to shoulder seam, sew sleeves to back and fronts. Join side and sleeve seams. Sew buttonhole band into place and invisibly seam centre back neck.

Chart 1

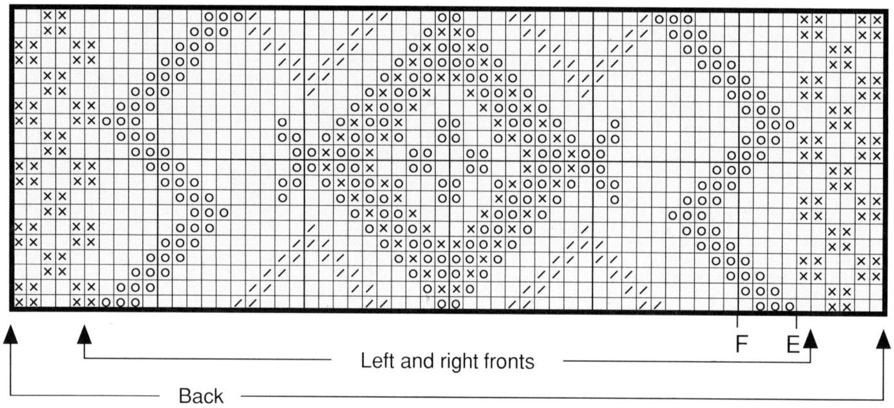

Left and right fronts

Back

F E

Chart 2

I H

Chart 3

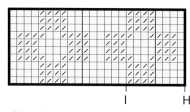

G

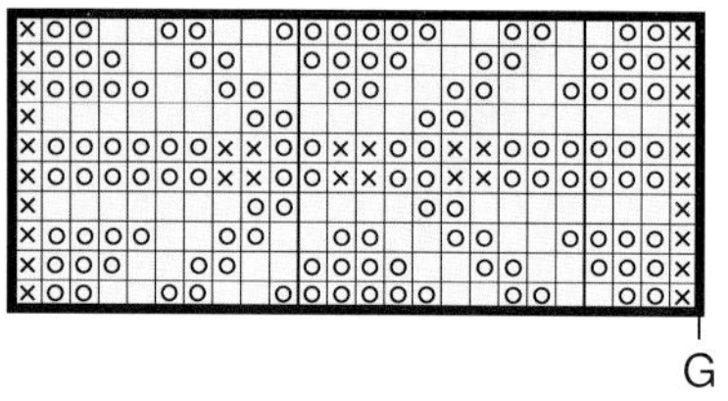

Key

☐	= Petrol
Ⓞ	= Red
☒	= Gingy
⟋	= Mustard
E	= begin chart for left front
F	= begin chart for right front
G	= begin chart for fronts
H	= begin chart for left front (top)
I	= begin chart for right front (top)

FLOWER GARDEN JACKET

This long-line jacket is very easy to knit and extremely wearable. The simple motif is repeated in different colourways, which can be chosen to match those of your wardrobe.

SIZE To fit bust 91–107cm (36–42in). Actual size: 118cm (46½in) bust; 84cm (33in) long; 67cm (26½in) sleeve.

MATERIALS Melinda Coss Mohair: Black (M) 600gm, Red (A) 25gm, Jade (B) 35gm, Mauve (C) 35gm, Yellow (D) 25gm. 6 buttons.

NEEDLES One pair of 4½mm (no. 7) needles and one pair of 5½mm (no. 5) needles.

TENSION Using 5½mm (no. 5) needles and measured over st st, 16 sts and 21 rows = 10cm square (4in square).

BACK

Using 4½mm (no. 7) needles and M, cast on 98 sts. Work in single rib for 6cm (2¼in).
Change to 5½mm (no. 5) needles and begin working from chart in st st for 104 rows. **Shape armholes.**
Cast off 6 sts at beg of the next 2 rows, then dec 1 st at beg of every row until 28 sts remain. Cast off.

LEFT FRONT

Using 4½mm (no. 7) needles and M, cast on 46 sts. Work in single rib for 6cm (2¼in).
Change to 5½mm (no. 5) needles and begin working from chart, in st st for 93 rows. **Shape neck.**
Dec 1 st at beg of the next and every sixth row. **At the same time**, when 104 rows have been worked, **shape armhole.**
Cast off 6 sts at beg of the next row, then 1 st at beg of every alt row. Cont shaping neck and armhole until 9 sts remain. Then cont shaping armhole only until 1 st remains. Fasten off.

RIGHT FRONT

Work as given for left front, reversing the shapings.

LEFT SLEEVE

Using 4½mm (no. 7) needles and M, cast on 50 sts. Work in single rib for 6cm (2¼in).
Change to 5½mm (no. 5) needles and begin working from chart, increasing 1 st each end of every fourth row for 76 rows. Work straight for 9 rows, **shape top.**
Dec 1 st each end of the next 4 rows.
Next row: *dec 1 st, knit to end.
Next row: purl to last 2 sts, p2tog.*
Repeat from * to * until 5 sts remain. Cast off.

RIGHT SLEEVE

Work as given for left sleeve up to **shape top**, then reverse the decreasing instructions.

LEFT COLLAR AND BUTTONBAND

Using 4½mm (no. 7) needles and M, cast on 178 sts. Work in single rib for 4cm (1½in). Cast off 94 sts, cont in rib. Dec 5 sts at beg of next and every alt row for 28 rows. Cast off remaining sts.

RIGHT COLLAR AND BUTTONHOLE BAND

Work as for left collar for 2cm (¾in).
Next row: rib 4, *cast off 3 sts, rib 15.
Repeat from * until 6 buttonholes have been completed. Rib to end of row.
Next row: work back across row casting on 3 sts over those cast off previously.
Cont in rib for a further 2cm (¾in), ending at buttonhole end.
Cast off 94 sts and cont as for left collar.

MAKING UP

Sew in sleeves to back and front pieces. Join sleeve and side seams, sew in collar around neck edge.

Sleeve

Key

☐ = Main colour (Black)

☒ = A (Red)

⬤ = B (Jade)

⊙ = C (Mauve)

▨ = D (Yellow)

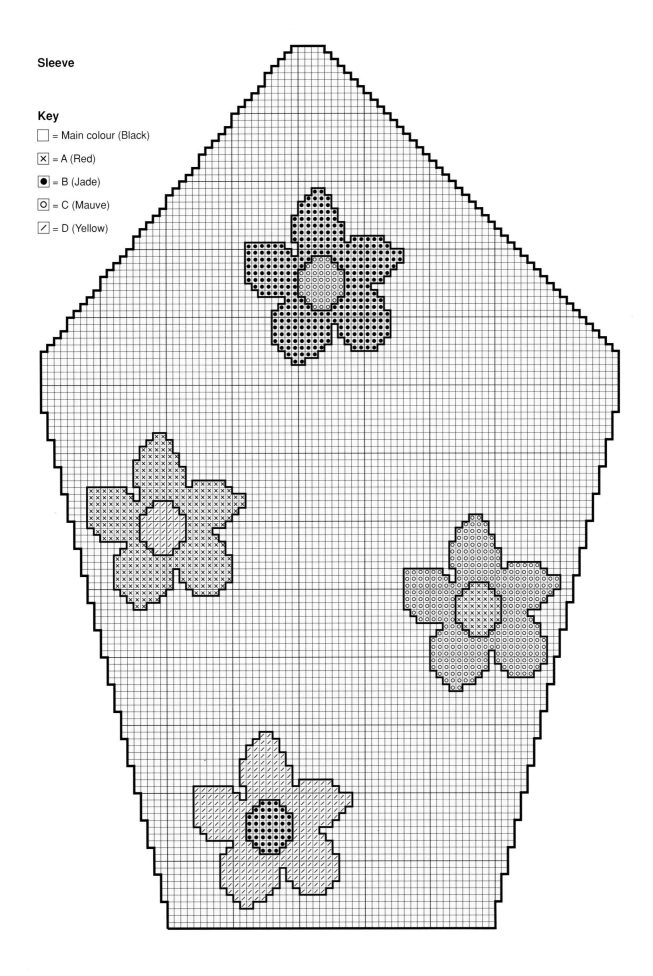

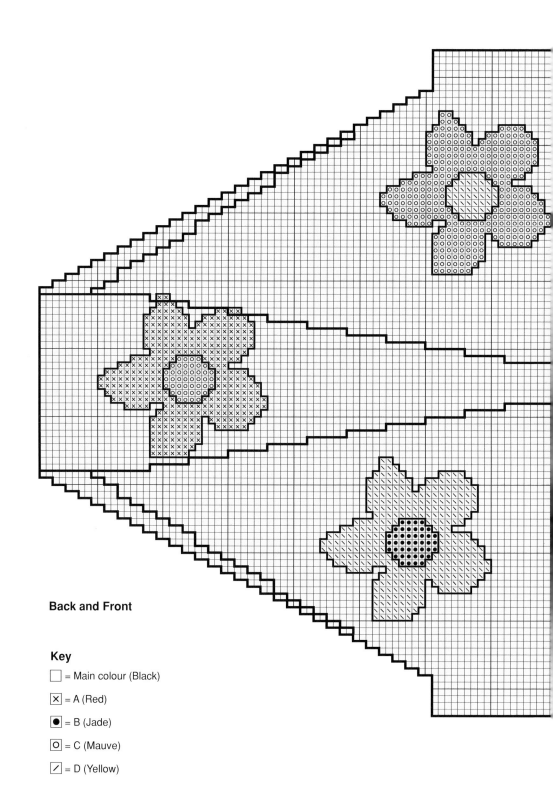

Back and Front

Key

☐ = Main colour (Black)

☒ = A (Red)

⬤ = B (Jade)

◯ = C (Mauve)

╱ = D (Yellow)

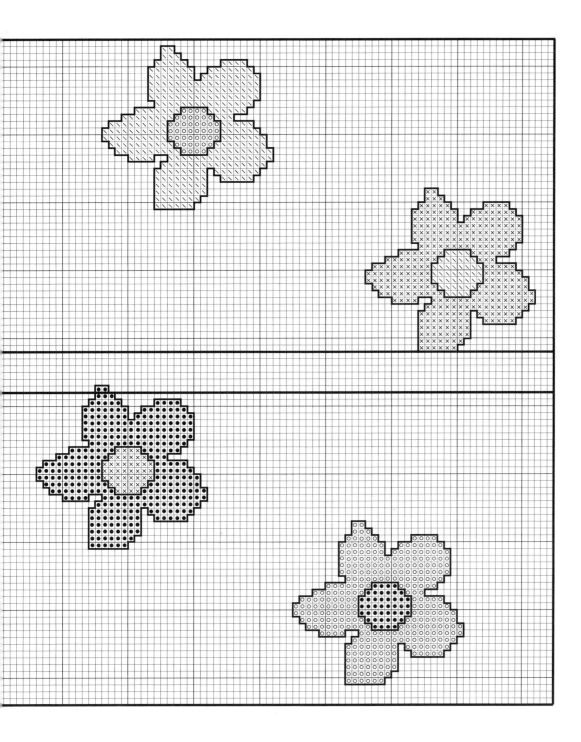

CUT-A-DASH JACKET

This smart jacket has a narrow shawl collar and a simple repeat motif. It was based on a Thirties textile design, and I love the contrast of the clear jewel colours against a black background. Work using the intarsia method (see p. 8).

SIZE To fit bust 86–102cm (34–40in). Actual size: 127cm (50in) bust; 63cm (25in) long; 44.5cm (17¹/₂in) sleeve.

MATERIALS Melinda Coss Mohair: Black (A) 425gm, Purple 60gm, Royal 75gm, Fuchsia 85gm, Jade 80gm. 4 buttons.

NEEDLES One pair 5¹/₂mm (no. 5) needles and one pair 4¹/₂mm (no. 7) needles.

TENSION Using 5¹/₂mm (no. 5) needles and measured over st st, 17 sts and 19 rows = 10cm square (4in square).

BACK

Using 4¹/₂mm (no. 7) needles and A, cast on 77 sts and work in single rib for 10cm (4in), increasing 31 sts evenly across last row of rib (108 sts).
Change to 5¹/₂mm (no. 5) needles and, using A and beg with a knit row, work 4 rows in st st.
Begin working from chart, repeating 6 times in all across row. When the 17 rows of chart are complete, start again from row 1, but work areas marked C in jade and areas marked B in purple.

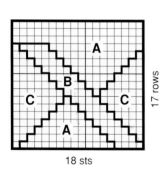

18 sts

Key

First 17 rows:
A = Black
B = Royal
C = Fuchsia

Second 17 rows:
A = Black
B = Purple
C = Jade

Repeat these 34 rows twice more, then repeat the first 15 rows. Continuing in A, **shape shoulders.**
Cast off 19 sts at the beg of the next 2 rows, then cast off remaining 70 sts.

LEFT FRONT

Using 4¹/₂mm (no. 7) needles and A, cast on 39 sts and work in single rib for 10cm (4in), increasing 15 sts evenly across last row of rib (54 sts).
Change to 5¹/₂mm (no. 5) needles and, starting with a knit row, st st 4 rows in A. Begin working from chart, repeating 3 times in all across row, and continue in colour sequence as set for back until 65 rows have been worked from beginning of st st. **Shape neck.**
Next row: keeping in pattern, p2tog, purl to end.
Cont working from chart, dec 1 st at neck edge on every foll third row until you have 37 sts (you are now on your seventh repeat of the chart). Work straight until you have completed 16 rows of the chart. **Shape shoulder.**
Cast off 19 sts at the beg of the next row, work 1 row, cast off remaining 18 sts.

RIGHT FRONT

Work as for left front but begin your neck shaping at the **end** of row 65, instead of at the beginning, and work 15 rows of chart before shaping shoulder instead of 16 rows.

SLEEVES

(Both alike.) Using 4¹/₂mm (no. 7) needles and A, cast on 45 sts and work in single rib for 14cm (5¹/₂in), inc 10 sts evenly across last row of charts (55 sts).
Change to 5¹/₂mm (no. 5) needles and, starting with a knit row, work 4 rows st st in A.
Begin working from chart placing as follows. Inc 1 in A, k1C, *k4B, k13A, k1C, repeat from * twice more, inc 1 in A. This sets your position for the chart.
Repeat chart 3 times in all, working colour sequence as for back. **At the same time** inc 1 st each end of every fourth row until you have 81 sts. When third repeat of chart is complete, work 3 extra rows in black. Cast off loosely.

RIGHT FRONT BAND

Join shoulders. Using 4¹/₂mm (no. 7) needles and A, cast on 14 sts. Work 10 rows in garter st (knit every row), **then make buttonhole.**
Next row: k6, cast off 2 sts, knit to end.
Next row: k6, cast on 2 sts, knit to end.
Knit 24 rows then repeat the two buttonhole rows. Repeat the last 26 rows twice more. **Shape collar.**
Knit to last 3 sts, k1, p1, k1 into next stitch, k2. Knit 3 rows, repeat the last 4 rows until you have 44 sts. Work straight until the band reaches the centre back neck. Cast off.

LEFT FRONT BAND

Work as for right front band omitting the buttonholes, and working collar shaping increases on the third stitch from beg of the row.

MAKING UP

Join shoulder seams. Invisibly seam cast-off edges of collar bands together, sew bands to fronts (shaped edge to neck edge) with collar seam at centre back. Join sleeves to jacket, join side and sleeve seams using narrow backstitch.

FLAGSHIP JACKET

I designed this jacket during the Gulf War when I was feeling particularly patriotic. It is a simple fairisle motif (see p. 9) and looks equally smart in autumn browns and greens.

SIZE To fit bust 86–102cm (34–40in). Actual size: 112cm (44in) bust; 70cm (27½in) long; 44cm (17¼in) sleeve.

MATERIALS Melinda Coss Mohair: Crimson 360gm, White 135gm, Royal 100gm. 4 buttons.

NEEDLES One pair of 4½mm (no. 7) needles and one pair of 5½mm (no. 5) needles.

TENSION Using 5½mm (no. 5) needles and measured over st st, 17 sts and 19 rows = 10cm square (4in square).

BACK

Using 4½mm (no. 7) needles and crimson, cast on 77 sts. Work in k1, p1 rib for 10cm (4in), inc 19 sts evenly across last row of rib (96 sts).
Change to 5½mm (no. 5) needles and begin following chart in st st, until the 44 rows are complete. Then repeat chart starting at row 5.
When this repeat is complete, start at row 5 once more and continue until you have completed the last crimson stripe. Continue in crimson, casting off 16 sts at beg of the next 4 rows. Cast off remaining 32 sts.

RIGHT FRONT

Using 4½mm (no. 7) needles and crimson, cast on 39 sts and work in k1, p1 rib for 10cm (4in), inc 9 sts across last row of rib (48 sts).
Change to 5½mm (no. 5) needles and begin following chart in st st, repeating from row 5 as for back until 65 rows have been worked. **Shape neck.**
Row 66 (WS): continuing to follow chart, purl to last 2 sts, p2tog.
Cont in pattern, dec 1 st at neck edge every foll third row until you have 32 sts.
Continue until you have completed the last crimson stripe. **Shape shoulder.**
Next row (WS): keeping in crimson, cast off 16 sts at beg of the row.
Work 1 row, cast off remaining 16 sts.

LEFT FRONT

Work as for right front but start neck shaping at the beginning of row 66 instead of the end, and start shoulder shaping at the beginning of a knit row (i.e. on row 4 of last crimson stripe).

SLEEVES

(Both alike.) Using 4½mm (no. 7) needles and crimson, cast on 45 sts. Work in k1, p1 rib for 10cm (4in), inc 7 sts across last row of rib (52 sts).
Change to 5½mm (no. 5) needles and begin following chart, starting on row 3, after dotted line, as indicated. **At the same time**, inc 1 st each end of every fourth row 13 times (78 sts). When chart is complete, begin again at row 5. When shapings are complete, continue straight for 12 rows, ending on a royal stripe. Cast off loosely in royal.
Join shoulder seams.

RIGHT FRONT BAND

Using 4½mm (no. 7) needles and crimson, cast on 14 sts. Work 10 rows in single rib, then **make buttonhole.**
Next row: rib 6, cast off 2 sts, rib to end.

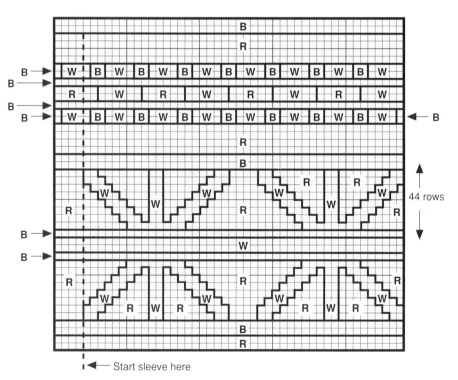

← Start sleeve here

Key
R = Crimson   B = Royal   W = White

Next row: rib 6, cast on 2 sts, rib to end.
Rib 24 rows then repeat the two buttonhole rows. Repeat the last 26 rows twice more. **Shape collar.**
Rib to last 3 sts, k1, p1, k1 into next stitch, rib 2. Rib 3 rows, repeat the last 4 rows until you have 44 sts. Work straight until the band reaches the centre back neck. Cast off.

LEFT FRONT BAND
Work as for right front band omitting the buttonholes and working collar shaping increases on the third stitch from beg of the row.

MAKING UP
Join shoulder seams. Invisibly seam cast-off edges of collar bands together, sew bands to fronts, shaped edge to neck edge with collar seam at centre back. Join sleeves to jacket, join side and sleeve seams using narrow backstitch.

Soft Option Jacket

A very classic option based on the Chanel jacket shape. The yarn should be stranded across the back and caught every five or six stitches. Do not use fairisle for this design, as the fabric will be too dense and the colours will show through behind the cream. No chart for this one.

> **Size** To fit bust 91–102cm (36–40in). Actual size: 110.5cm (43½in) bust; 72cm (28¼in) long; 51.5cm (20¼in) sleeve seam.
>
> **Materials** Melinda Coss Mohair: Cream (cr) 200gm, Pink (pk) 150gm, Silver (s) 260gm. 7 gilt buttons.
>
> **Needles** One pair of 5½mm (no. 5) needles and one pair of 5mm (no. 6) needles. Stitch holder.
>
> **Tension** Using 5½mm (no. 5) needles and measured over pattern, 15 sts and 17 rows = 10cm square (4in square).

Back

Using 5mm (no. 6) needles and cream, cast on 84 sts and knit 2 rows.
Change to 5½mm (no. 5) needles and work in st st in pattern as follows.
Row 1: 13 s, 1 cr, 13s, 1 cr, 13 s, 2 cr, 13 s, 1 cr, 13 s, 1 cr, 13 s.
Row 2: 1 cr, 11 s, 3 cr, 11 s, 3 cr, 11 s, 4 cr, 11 s, 3 cr, 11 s, 3 cr, 11 s, 1 cr.
Row 3: 2 cr, 9 s, 5 cr, 9 s, 5 cr, 9 s, 6 cr, 9 s, 5 cr, 9 s, 5 cr, 9 s, 2 cr.
Row 4: 3 cr, 7 s, 7 cr, 7 s, 7 cr, 7 s, 8 cr, 7 s, 7 cr, 7 s, 7 cr, 7 s, 3 cr.
Row 5: 4 cr, 5 s, 9 cr, 5 s, 9 cr, 5 s, 10 cr, 5 s, 9 cr, 5 s, 9 cr, 5 s, 4 cr.
Row 6: 5 cr, 3 s, 11 cr, 3 s, 11 cr, 3 s, 12 cr, 3 s, 11 cr, 3 s, 11 cr, 3 s, 5 cr.
Rows 7 and 8: 6 cr, 1 s, 13 cr, 1 s, 13 cr, 1 s, 14 cr, 1 s, 13 cr, 1 s, 13 cr, 1 s, 6 cr.
Rows 9–14: as row 6 back to row 1, in that reverse order.
Rows 15–28: as rows 1–14, but using pink, instead of cream.
These 28 rows form a repeat of the diamond pattern. Work in pattern a further 40 rows. **Shape armholes.**
Cast off 7 sts at beg of each of the next 2 rows (70 sts). Work in pattern a further 46 rows. **Slope shoulders.**
Cast off 10 sts at beg of each of the next 2 rows, then 9 sts at beg of each of the foll 2 rows. Leave remaining 32 sts on a spare needle.

Pocket linings

(Both alike.) Using 5½mm (no. 5) needles and pink, cast on 20 sts and, beginning with a knit row, st st 26 rows. Leave sts on a st holder.

Left front

Using 5mm (no. 6) needles and cream, cast on 42 sts and knit 2 rows.
Change to 5½mm (no. 5) needles and work in pattern as follows.
Row 1: *13 s, 1 cr, repeat from * twice more.
Row 2: 2 cr, 11 s, 3 cr, 11 s, 3 cr, 11 s, 1 cr.
Row 3: 2 cr, 9 s, 5 cr, 9 s, 5 cr, 9 s, 3 cr.
Row 4: 4 cr, 7 s, 7 cr, 7 s, 7 cr, 7 s, 3 cr.
Row 5: 4 cr, 5 s, 9 cr, 5 s, 9 cr, 5 s, 5 cr.
Row 6: 6 cr, 3 s, 11 cr, 3 s, 11 cr, 3 s, 5 cr.
Row 7: 6 cr, 1 s, 13 cr, 1 s, 13 cr, 1 s, 7 cr.
Row 8: 7 cr, 1 s, 13 cr, 1 s, 13 cr, 1 s, 6 cr.
Row 9: 5 cr, 3 s, 11 cr, 3 s, 11 cr, 3 s, 6 cr.
Row 10: 5 cr, 5 s, 9 cr, 5 s, 9 cr, 5 s, 4 cr.
Row 11: 3 cr, 7 s, 7 cr, 7 s, 7 cr, 7 s, 4 cr.
Row 12: 3 cr, 9 s, 5 cr, 9 s, 5 cr, 9 s, 2 cr.
Row 13: 1 cr, 11 s, 3 cr, 11 s, 3 cr, 11 s, 2 cr.
Row 14: *1 cr, 13 s, repeat from * twice more.
Work in pattern a further 14 rows, using pink instead of cream.
These 28 rows form a repeat of the pattern for the left front.
Pocket row: pattern 15, slip next 20 sts on to a st holder and leave at front of work and, in their place, pattern across the 20 sts of one pocket lining, pattern 7.
Work in pattern a further 39 rows. **Shape armhole.**
Cast off 7 sts, pattern to end (35 sts). Work in pattern a further 32 rows. **Shape neck.**
Cast off 10 sts at beg of the next row, then dec 1 st at neck edge on each of the next 6 rows (19 sts). Work in pattern a further 8 rows. **Slope shoulder.**
Cast off 10 sts at beg of the next row (9 sts). Work in pattern 1 row. Cast off.

Right front

Using 5mm (no. 6) needles and cream, cast on 42 sts and knit 2 rows.
Change to 5½mm (no. 5) needles and work in pattern as follows.
Row 1: 1 cr, 13 s, 1 cr, 13 s, 1 cr, 13 s.
Row 2: 1 cr, 11 s, 3 cr, 11 s, 3 cr, 11 s, 2 cr.
Row 3: 3 cr, 9 s, 5 cr, 9 s, 5 cr, 9 s, 2 cr.
Row 4: 3 cr, 7 s, 7 cr, 7 s, 7 cr, 7 s, 4 cr.
Row 5 (buttonhole row): 2 cr, yfwd, k2tog with cr, knit 1 more cr, 5 s, 9 cr, 5 s, 9 cr, 5 s, 4 cr.
Row 6: 5 cr, 3 s, 11 cr, 3 s, 11 cr, 3 s, 6 cr.
Row 7: 7 cr, 1 s, 13 cr, 1 s, 13 cr, 1 s, 6 cr.
Row 8: 6 cr, 1 s, 13 cr, 1 s, 13 cr, 1 s, 7 cr.
Row 9: 6 cr, 3 s, 11 cr, 3 s, 11 cr, 3 s, 5 cr.
Row 10: 4 cr, 5 s, 9 cr, 5 s, 9 cr, 5 s, 5 cr.
Row 11: 4 cr, 7 s, 7 cr, 7 s, 7 cr, 7 s, 3 cr.

Row 12: 2 cr, 9 s, 5 cr, 9 s, 5 cr, 9 s, 3 cr.
Row 13: 2 cr, 11 s, 3 cr, 11 s, 3 cr, 11 s, 1 cr.
Row 14: *13 s, 1 cr, repeat from * twice more.
Work in pattern a further 14 rows, using pink instead of cream, and making a buttonhole on the seventh of these rows. These 28 rows form a repeat of the pattern for the right front. **Shape neck.** Cast off 10 sts at beg of the next row, then dec 1 st at neck edge on each of the next 6 rows (19 sts). Work in pattern a further 8 rows. **Slope shoulders.**
Cast off 10 sts at beg of the next row (9 sts). Work in pattern 1 row. Cast off.

SLEEVES

(Both alike.) Using 5mm (no. 6) needles and cream, cast on 40 sts and knit 2 rows.
Change to 5½mm (no. 5) needles and work in pattern as follows.
Row 1: 5 s, 1 cr, 13 s, 2 cr, 13 s, 1 cr, 5 s.
Row 2: 4 s, 3 cr, 11 s, 4 cr, 11 s, 3 cr, 4 s.
Row 3: 3 s, 5 cr, 9 s, 6 cr, 9 s, 5 cr, 3 s.
Row 4: 2 s, 7 cr, 7 s, 8 cr, 7 s, 7 cr, 2 s.
Row 5: inc with s, 9 cr, 5 s, 10 cr, 5 s, 9 cr, inc with s (42 sts).
Row 6: 1 s, 11 cr, 3 s, 12 cr, 3 s, 11 cr, 1 s.
Rows 7 and 8: 13 cr, 1 s, 14 cr, 1 s, 13 cr.
Row 9: inc with s, 11 cr, 3 s, 12 cr, 3 s, 11 cr, inc with s (44 sts).
Row 10: 3 s, 9 cr, 5 s, 10 cr, 5 s, 9 cr, 3 s.
Row 11: 4 s, 7 cr, 7 s, 8 cr, 7 s, 7 cr, 4 s.
Row 12: 5 s, 5 cr, 9 s, 6 cr, 9 s, 5 cr, 5 s.
Row 13: inc with s, knit 5 more s, 3 cr, 11 s, 4 cr, 11 s, 3 cr, 5 s, inc with s (46 sts).
Row 14: 8 s, 1 cr, 13 s, 2 cr, 13 s, 1 cr, 8 s.
Maintaining continuity of the pattern to match back and taking extra sts into the pattern as they occur, work in pattern a further 2 rows, then inc 1 st at each end of the next row and the 17 foll fourth rows (82 sts).
Mark each end of last row, to denote end of sleeve seam. Work in pattern a further 7 rows. Cast off.

RIGHT FRONT BORDER

First join shoulder seams. With RS of work facing and using 5mm (no. 6) needles and cream, pick up and knit 74 sts evenly up right front and knit 2 rows. Cast off.

LEFT FRONT BORDER

With RS of work facing and using 5mm (no. 6) needles and cream, pick up and knit 74 sts evenly down left front and knit 2 rows. Cast off.

NECKBAND

With RS of work facing and using 5mm (no. 6) needles and cream, pick up and knit 24 sts up right front neck edge, knit across the 32 sts at back neck, then pick up and knit 24 sts down left front neck edge (80 sts). Knit 2 rows. Cast off.

POCKET TOPS

(Both alike.) With RS of work facing and using 5mm (no. 6)

needles and cream, knit across the 20 sts from one st holder. Knit 1 row. Cast off.

MAKING UP

Do not press. Sew cast-off edge of sleeves to straight row-ends of armholes, then sew straight row-ends of armholes, then sew straight row-ends above markers on sleeves to cast-off groups at underarms on back and fronts. Join sleeve and side seams, matching pattern. Sew down pocket linings on the wrong side and row-ends of pocket tops on the right side. Sew on buttons to correspond with buttonholes.

REFLECTIONS JACKET

Bright, bold paintbox colours make this jacket a show-stopper. It consists of one small repeating chart. Strand the yarn not in use loosely across the back of the work, catching it every four or five stitches. This is a jacket for all seasons.

SIZE To fit bust 81–102cm (32–40in). Actual size: 126cm (49½in) bust; 77cm (30¼in) long; 41cm (16in) sleeve.

MATERIALS Melinda Coss Mohair: Black (main colour A) 450gm, Emerald 80gm, Yellow 85gm, Lavender 50gm, Scarlet 60gm. 4 buttons.

NEEDLES One pair of 4½mm (no. 7) needles and one pair of 5½mm (no. 5) needles.

TENSION Using 5½mm (no. 5) needles and measured over st st, 17 sts and 19 rows = 10cm square (4in square).

BACK

Using 4½mm (no. 7) needles and A, cast on 78 sts. Work in k1, p1 rib for 2 rows, change to scarlet, rib 4 rows, change to A, cont in rib until work measures 10cm (4in), inc 26 sts evenly across last row (104 sts).
Change to 5½mm (no. 5) needles and begin foll chart, reading B as emerald. Repeat chart 4 times across row. When 30 rows of chart are complete, start again at row 1, reading B as yellow. On the third repeat read B as lavender, and on the last repeat read B as scarlet. When the fourth repeat is complete, **shape shoulders.** Using A, cast off 17 sts at the beginning of the next 4 rows, then cast off remaining 36 sts.

LEFT FRONT

Using 4½mm (no. 7) needles and A, cast on 40 sts. Work in k1, p1 rib for 2 rows, change to scarlet, rib 4 rows, change to A, cont in rib until work measures 10cm (4in), increasing 12 sts evenly across last row (52 sts).
Change to 5½mm (no. 5) needles and begin foll chart, repeating twice across row. Continue in colour sequence as for back. **At the same time** on the seventh row of the third pattern repeat, **shape neck** by dec 1 st at the end of this row and then, keeping in pattern, dec 1 st at the same edge on every foll third row 17 times (34 sts).

NB When working the last stitch at neck edge on the final 7 rows of the last pattern repeat, remain in A. When fourth pattern repeat is complete, work 2 rows in A then **shape shoulder.**
Cast off 17 sts in A, work 1 row A, cast off remaining 17 sts.

RIGHT FRONT

Work as for left front, reversing shaping.

SLEEVES

(Both alike.) Using 4½mm (no. 7) needles and A, cast on 46 sts. Work in k1, p1 rib for 2 rows, change to scarlet, rib 4 rows, change to A, cont in rib until work measures 8cm (3in), inc 6 sts evenly across last row (52 sts).Change to 5½mm (no.5) needles. Next row (RS): begin working from chart, repeating twice across row and working contrast B in emerald for the first 30 rows and in yellow for the second 30 rows. **At the same time** increase 1 st each end of the third row, the 2 foll third rows and then every fourth row until you have 82 sts. Work extra sts in pattern – see note below. When second repeat of chart is complete, work 3 rows in black, then cast off loosely in black.

NB When increasing sleeve sts at beg of a RS row, read the first st of the same row at the **left** edge of the chart; for the second increase at the same edge, read the second st at the **left** edge of chart, etc.
Join shoulder seams.

LEFT FRONT BAND AND HALF COLLAR

Using 4½mm (no. 7) needles and A, cast on 12 sts. Work in rib until band fits, when slightly stretched, to beginning of neck shaping, ending with a WS row. **Shape collar.**
Next row (RS): rib to last 3 sts, k1, p1, k1 into next st, rib to end.

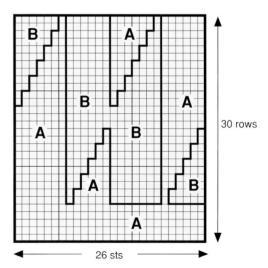

30 rows

26 sts

Key
A = Black (main colour)
B = Contrast colour as given in pattern

Rib 5 rows, repeat the last 6 rows 7 times more (30 sts). Work straight in rib until band reaches centre back neck, cast off. Slipstitch band into position on left front.

With pins, mark positions for 4 buttons, the first 10 rows up from the bottom of the rib, and the last just below the beginning of the collar shaping, with the other 2 spaced evenly in between.

RIGHT FRONT BAND AND HALF COLLAR

Join shoulders. Using 4½mm (no. 7) needles and A, cast on 12 sts. Work 10 rows in k1, p1 rib, then **make buttonhole.**

Next row: rib 4, cast off 2, rib 4.

Next row: rib 4, cast on 2, rib 4.

Cont as for left front band, making buttonholes to correspond with the positions of the pins and reversing collar shaping (i.e. work increases on the third stitch from the beginning of the row). When band is complete, cast off and slipstitch into position on right front, then invisibly seam short ends together at centre back neck.

MAKING UP

Join sleeves to jacket, join side and sleeve seams.

SPLASH OF PINK COAT

Simple triangles in three shades of pink add a touch of glamour to this elegant navy coat. It is simple to knit using the intarsia method (see p. 8).

SIZE To fit bust 86–102cm (34–40in). Actual size: 130cm (51in) bust; 102cm (40in) long; 43cm (17in) sleeve with cuff folded back.

MATERIALS Melinda Coss Mohair: Navy (main colour) 650gm, Fuchsia (A) 50gm, Candyfloss (B) 40gm, Pink (C) 30gm. 8 buttons.

NEEDLES One pair of 4¹/₂mm (no. 7) needles and one pair of 5¹/₂mm (no. 5) needles. Safety pins.

TENSION Using 5¹/₂mm (no. 5) needles and measured over st st, 16 sts and 20 rows = 10cm square (4in square).

BACK

Using 4¹/₂mm (no. 7) needles and main colour, cast on 91 sts. Work in k1, p1 rib as follows.
Row 1 (RS): k1, (p1, k1) rep to end.
Row 2: p1, (k1, p1) rep to end.
Rep these 2 rows until rib measures 10cm (4in), finishing with a WS row and inc on last row of rib as follows: rib 3, (inc into next st, rib 6) rep to last 4 sts, inc into next st, rib to end (104 sts).
Change to 5¹/₂mm (no. 5) needles and, working in st st throughout and starting with a knit row, beg to follow chart for back, working triangles in positions as shown. Complete the 178 rows of the chart as indicated, then **shape shoulders.**
Row 179 (RS): cast off 8 sts at the beg of the row and work to end.
Row 180: cast off 8 sts at the beg of the row and work to end.
Row 181: cast off 8 sts at the beg of the row, work 22 sts, cast off 28 sts, work to end. Starting with the left side, work each side separately.
Row 182: cast off 8 sts at the beg of row and work to end.
Row 183: cast off 2 sts at neck edge and work to end.
Row 184: cast off 9 sts at the beg of row and work to end.
Row 185: cast off 2 sts at neck edge and work to end. Cast off rem 9 sts.
With RS facing, rejoin yarn to right side of neck and complete to match left side, reversing all shaping.

LEFT FRONT

Using 4¹/₂mm (no. 7) needles and main colour, cast on 55 sts. Work in k1, p1 rib as for back until rib measures 10cm (4in), ending with WS row and inc across last row of rib as follows: rib 10 and leave these sts on a safety pin, rib 4, (inc into next st, rib 5) rep to last 5 sts, inc into next st, rib to end (52 sts).
Change to 5¹/₂mm (no. 5) needles and, working in st st throughout, beg to follow chart for left front. Work until 165 rows have been completed then **shape neck.**
Row 166 (WS): cast off 8 sts and work to end.
Then dec 1 st at neck edge on next 10 rows (34 sts). Cont straight until row 178 of chart has been worked then **shape shoulder.**
Row 179 (RS): cast off 8 sts and work to end.
Row 180: purl.
Row 181: cast off 8 sts and work to end.
Row 182: purl.
Row 183: cast off 9 sts and work to end.
Row 184: purl. Cast off rem 9 sts.

Sleeve

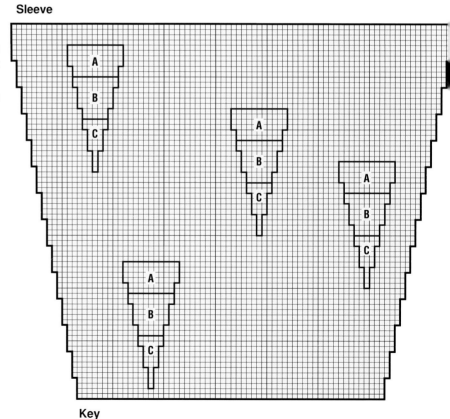

Key

☐ = Navy (main colour) B = Candyfloss

A = Fuchsia C = Pink

RIGHT FRONT

Work rib as for left front but make a buttonhole 3cm (1¼in) up from cast-on edge as follows.

Next row (RS): rib 4, yon, k2tog, rib to end.

On return row cast on 1 st over cast-off st on previous row. Cont in rib until work measures 10cm (4in), ending with a RS row.

Next row (WS): rib 4, (inc into next st, rib 5) rep to last 15 sts, inc into next st, rib to end.

Change to 5½mm (no. 5) needles and, leaving first 10 sts on a safety pin for buttonhole band (52 sts) and working in st st throughout, beg to follow chart for right front until row 166 of chart has been completed. Then **shape neck.**

Row 167 (RS): cast off 8 sts and work to end.

Then dec 1 st at neck edge on next 10 rows (34 sts). Work straight until row 178 of chart has been completed, then **shape shoulder.**

Row 179 (RS): knit.

Row 180: cast off 8 sts and work to end.

Row 181: knit.

Row 182: cast off 8 sts and work to end.

Row 183: knit.

Row 184: cast off 9 sts and work to end.

Cast off rem 9 sts.

SLEEVES

(Both alike.) Using 4½mm (no. 7) needles and main colour, cast on 49 sts. Work in k1, p1 rib as for back for 10cm (4in), ending with a WS row, and inc on last row of rib as follows: rib 4, (inc into next st, rib 3) rep to last 5 sts, inc into next st, rib to end (60 sts).

Change to 5½mm (no. 5) needles and, working in st st throughout, beg to follow chart for sleeves, inc 1 st each end of every fifth row until there are 86 sts. Work straight until chart is complete and cast off loosely.

BUTTONBAND

Using 4½mm (no. 7) needles and main colour and with RS of left front facing, slip 10 sts held on safety pin on to left-hand needle and work as follows.

Row 1: knit into front and back of first st, rib to end (11 sts). Work in rib until buttonband, slightly stretched, reaches start of neck shaping. Leave stitches on a safety pin for collar. Slipstitch the buttonband into place along edge of left front. Use pins to mark positions for 6 evenly spaced buttons (the seventh buttonhole has already been worked on the rib, and the eighth buttonhole will be placed on the collar, 6cm (2½in) up from the neck shaping).

BUTTONHOLE BAND

Using 4½mm (no. 7) needles and main colour and with RS of right front facing, slip 10 sts from safety pin on to left-hand needle and work as follows.

Row 1: rib to last st, work into front and back of st (11 sts). Work in rib until buttonhole band, slightly stretched, reaches

start of neck shaping, **at the same time** making buttonholes as described in instructions for left front rib to correspond with the pins on buttonband. Leave sts on a safety pin. Slipstitch the buttonhole band into place along the edge of the right front. Use the main colour to join the shoulder seams with a flat seam.

COLLAR

Using 4½mm (no. 7) needles and main colour and with RSs facing, pick up and knit 11 sts from buttonhole band, 36 sts up right front neck shaping, 1 st from shoulder seam, 9 sts from back neck shaping, 35 sts across back neck, 9 sts from back neck shaping, 1 st from shoulder seam, 36 sts down left front neck shaping and 11 sts from buttonband (149 sts).

Work in k1, p1 rib for 6cm (2½in), then work buttonhole in line with those previously worked. Rib for another 6cm (2½in), then work another buttonhole. Rib for another 6cm (2½in), ending with a WS row. Cast off in rib. Fold collar in half and slipstitch to pick-up edge of collar.

MAKING UP

Using main colour and flat stitch, sew sleeves to shoulder seam, then join side and sleeve seams. Sew on buttons.

Key

☐ = Navy (main colour)　B = Candyfloss

A = Fuchsia　　　　　　C = Pink

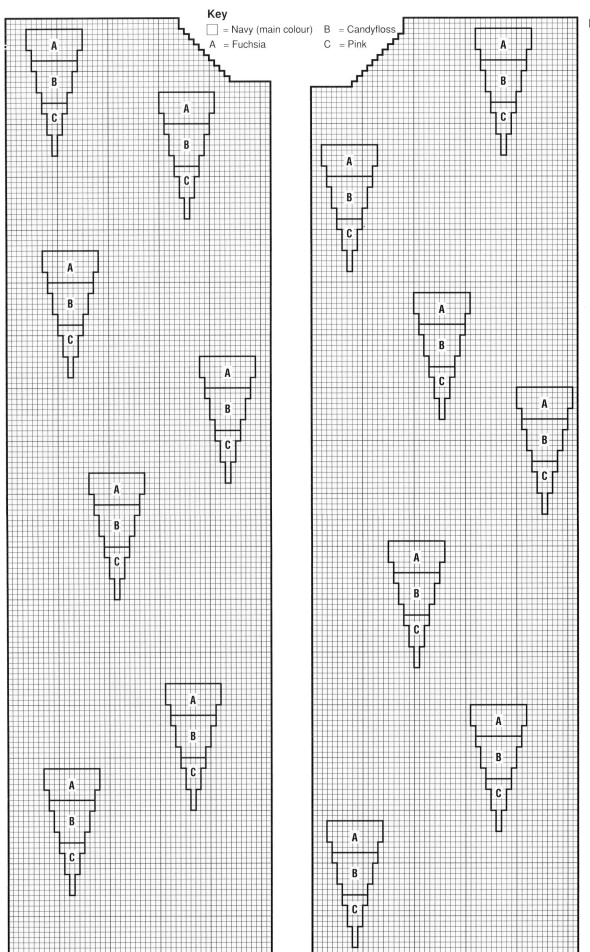

Back

79

Zigzag and Bobbles jacket

This jacket suits all age groups and looks classically smart. The bobbles add zing to the simple shape, but they can be left off if required, leaving a jacket that will look good at both work and play.

Size To fit bust 91 – 102cm (36 – 40in). Actual size: 120cm (47in) bust; 74cm (29in) long; 54cm (21in) sleeve seam.

Materials Melinda Coss Mohair: Navy (M) 450gm, Fuchsia (A) 220gm, Lemon (B) 110gm, Jade (C) 120gm.

Needles One pair 5¹/₂in (no. 5) needles.

Tension Using 5¹/₂mm (no. 5) needles and measured over pattern, 16 sts and 21 rows = 10cm square (4in square).

NB MB = make bobble: k5 times into the next st, turn, (p5, turn, k5) twice, turn, p2tog, p1, p2tog, turn, slip 1, p2, psso.

Back

Using 5¹/₂mm (no. 5) needles and M, cast on 96 sts. Starting with a knit row, work in st st for 10 rows.
Row 11: k3, * MB using A, k4, rep from * to last 3 sts, k3.
St st 3 rows then beg foll chart. Work straight until back measures 49cm (19¹/₄in). Place markers each end of row for armhole position. Cont until back measures 75cm (29¹/₂in) from start. **Shape shoulder.**
Cast off 18 sts at beg of next 4 rows. Cast off rem 24 sts.

Left front

Using 5¹/₂mm (no. 5) needles and M, cast on 48 sts. Work 10 rows as given for back.
Row 11: k4, * MB in A, k3, rep from * to last 4 sts, k4.
Work 3 rows in st st, then begin foll chart until front measures 42cm (16¹/₂in), ending with a RS row. **Shape neck.**
Dec 1 st at the beg of next and every eighth row until you have 36 sts. Cont straight until front measures 75cm (29¹/₂in), ending with a WS row. **Shape shoulder.**
Cast off 18 sts at beg of the next row, work 1 row, cast off rem 18 sts.

Right front

Work as for left front, reversing shapings.

Sleeves

(Both alike.) Using 5¹/₂mm (no. 5) needles and M, cast on 38 sts. Work 14 rows as given for back. Cont working from chart, inc 1

st at each end of every third row until you have 90 sts. Cont straight until sleeve measures 54cm (21¹/₄in). Cast off.

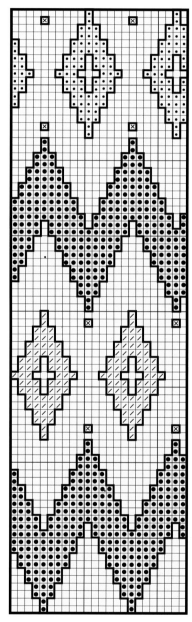

Key

☐	= M (Navy)	⊡	= B (Lemon)
⬤	= A (Fuchsia)	╱	= C (Jade)
☒	= Make bobble in Fuchsia		

RIGHT COLLAR AND BAND

Using 5½mm (no. 5) needles and M, cast on 10 sts. St st 4 rows.
Row 5: k7, MB using A, k2.
Row 6: purl.
Rep these 6 rows until band measures 40cm (15¾in), ending with a RS row. **Shape collar.**
Cast off 5 sts, cont on next 5 sts then cast on 5 sts. Cont making bobble on every sixth row, but on eighth st from left-hand edge (i.e. bobble remains in same position but facing is now on opposite side). **At the same time** beg inc as follows.
Row 1: p10.
Row 2: make 1 st, k10.
Row 3: p11.
Row 4: k11.
Row 5: p11.
Row 6: k1, make 1 st, k10.
Row 7: p12.
Row 8: k12.
Row 9: p12.
Row 10: k2, make 1 st, k10.
Row 11: p13.
Row 12: k13.
Cont working in this sequence, making a st every fourth row between collar and bobble band until you have 33 sts. Cont straight until collar measures 83cm (32½in), ending with a RS row. Cast off 5 sts at beg of next and every other row until all sts are decreased.

LEFT COLLAR AND BAND

Work as for right collar and band, reversing facing and shapings.

MAKING UP

Join shoulder seams. Sew in sleeves between markers. Join sleeve and side seams. Sew bobble band to front edge and collar around neck edge. Slipstitch down facing and hem of garment and sleeves.

Diamond jacket

This jacket shape covers everyone, and several of our customers have knitted this design in pastel shades to go with their summer wardrobes. It is the kind of shape and design that does not date and still remains high on the 'favourites' list.

SIZE To fit bust 86–102cm (34–40in). Actual size: 122cm (48in) bust; 69cm (27¹/₂in) long; 42cm (16¹/₂in) sleeve.

MATERIALS Melinda Coss Mohair: Black (A) 375gm, Royal (B) 100gm, Turquoise (C), Mauve (D), Emerald (E), Fuchsia (F), Yellow (G) and Scarlet (H), 50gm of each. 4 large buttons.

NEEDLES One pair of 4¹/₂mm (no. 7) needles and one pair of 5¹/₂mm (no. 5) needles.

TENSION Using 5¹/₂mm (no. 5) needles and measured over pattern, 17 sts and 19 rows =10cm square (4in square).

BACK

Using 4¹/₂mm (no. 7) needles and A, cast on 77 sts. Work in k1, p1 rib as follows. 4 rows A, 4 rows F, 4 rows A, 4 rows E and 3 rows A.*

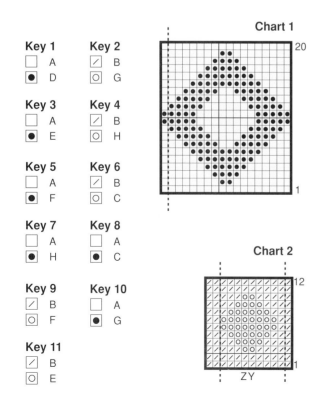

Key 1
☐ A
● D

Key 2
╱ B
○ G

Key 3
☐ A
● E

Key 4
╱ B
○ H

Key 5
☐ A
● F

Key 6
╱ B
○ C

Key 7
☐ A
● H

Key 8
☐ A
● C

Key 9
╱ B
○ F

Key 10
☐ A
● G

Key 11
╱ B
○ E

Chart 1
20

1

Chart 2
12

1

ZY

Next row: using A, rib 2 (inc 1, rib 2) rep to end (102 sts). Change to 5¹/₂mm (no. 5) needles.
**Work in st st, working pattern from chart 1 using key 1.
Row 1: using A, knit as first chart row, inc 1 st at centre.
Row 2: purl st before the dotted line, repeat 17 sts beyond dotted line to end.
Row 3: repeat 17 sts before dotted line to last st. Knit st beyond dotted line.
Cont in this way until 20th chart row is worked and dec 1 st at centre of last row.*** Cont in st st, working pattern from chart 2 using key 2 as follows. Knit 1 row and purl 1 row as first and second chart rows.
Row 3: k1 st before right dotted line of third chart row, *rep 9 sts between dotted lines** to last 2 sts, k2 sts beyond left dotted line.
Row 4: p2 sts before left dotted line of fourth chart row,* rep 9 sts between dotted lines ** to last st, purl st beyond right dotted line.
Cont in this way until 12th chart row is worked.****
Using key 3 instead of key 1 and key 4 instead of key 2, repeat from ** to ***.
Using key 5 instead of key 1 and key 6 instead of key 2, repeat from ** to ****.
Using key 7 instead of key 1, rep from ** to **** only. **Shape shoulders.**
Using A only, cast off 16 sts at beg of next 2 rows and 17 sts at beg of foll 2 rows. Cast off.

LEFT FRONT

Using 4¹/₂mm (no. 7) needles and A, cast on 39 sts. Rib as back to *.
Next row: (rib 2, inc 1) 12 times, rib 3 (51 sts).
Change to 5¹/₂mm (no. 5) needles and work from ** to *** of back. Cont in st st, working pattern from chart 2 using key 2 as follows. Knit 1 row and purl 1 row as first and second chart rows.****
Row 3: as third chart 2 row of back to ** and to last 5 sts, k5 sts beyond right dotted line ending level with Y.
Row 4: beg level with Y and p5 sts before right dotted line of fourth chart row, complete as fourth chart 2 row of back from *.
Cont in this way until 12-row chart is worked.
Using key 3 instead of key 1, repeat from ** to *** of back. To shape front, while working in pattern as set, changing colour as for back, at the same time dec 1 st at end of next row and at same edge on every foll third row to 34 sts. Cont straight until chart 1 pattern using key 7 is worked (33 sts). **Shape shoulder.**
Cont with A only, and cast off 16 sts at beg of next row. Work 1 row. Cast off.

RIGHT FRONT

Work as for left front to ****.
Row 3: beg level with Z and k4 sts before left dotted line of third chart row, work as third chart 2 row of back from *.
Row 4: as fourth chart 2 row of back to ** and to last 4 sts, p4 sts beyond left dotted line, ending level with Z.
Cont in pattern as set and complete to match left front.

SLEEVES

(Both alike.) Using 4½mm (no. 7) needles and A, cast on 45 sts. Work in k1, p1 rib stripes of 4 rows A, 4 rows C, 4 rows A, 4 rows G and 3 rows A.
Next row (WS): using A rib 4, inc 1, (rib 3, inc 1) 9 times, rib 4 (55 sts).
Change to 5½mm (no. 5) needles. Using key 8 instead of key 1, pattern as back from ** to *** with an extra 2A at each end of second row to position pattern, and **at the same time** inc 1 st each end of fifth chart row, then every foll fourth row, taking made sts into pattern at each side (63 sts).
Using key 9, inc 1 st each end of first row, work 2 rows of chart 2.
Row 3: k1F, beg level with Z and work 4 sts before left dotted line, rep 9 sts between dotted lines to last 6 sts, k5 sts beyond right dotted line, ending level with Y, k1F.
Cont in pattern as set, still inc each end of every fourth row until 12-row chart is worked (69 sts). Still inc as set to 81 sts, **at the same time** work patterns from chart 1 using key 10, and chart 2 using key 11, setting diamonds of each chart in line with previous patterns. Using B cast off loosely.

FRONT BANDS AND COLLAR

Join shoulders.
Right: using 4½mm (no. 7) needles and A, cast on 14 sts.
Beginning first row p1, work 10 rows in k1, p1 rib.
Buttonhole row: rib 6, cast off 2, rib 6.
Next row: rib 6, cast on 2, rib 6.
Rib 24 rows, then rep 2 buttonhole rows again. Rep last 26 rows twice more.*
Collar increase row: rib to last 3 sts (k1, p1, k1) all in next st, p1, k1.**
Rib 3 rows. Repeat last 4 rows to 44 sts. Cont straight until band and shaped edge of collar fits up front and across half of back neck to centre. Cast off ribwise.

Left: beg first row k1, work as right to * (omit buttonholes).
Collar increase row: k1, p1, (k1, p1 and k1) all in next st, rib to end.
Complete as right from **.

MAKING UP

Join cast-off ends of collar; placing seam to centre back, sew shaped edge of bands and collar up fronts and across back. Beg and end 24cm (9½in) from shoulder seams. Sew on sleeves. Join side and sleeve seams.

STRIKE UP THE BAND JACKET

Chevron stripes are extremely flattering, since they give the impression that you slope in at the waist, which is especially wonderful when you don't! This jacket is simple to knit and an easy shape to wear, which must account for its huge popularity.

SIZE To fit bust 86–102cm (34–40in). Actual size: 121cm (47½in) bust; 73cm (28¾in) long; 42.5cm (16¾in) sleeve seam.

MATERIALS Melinda Coss Mohair: Navy (M) 340gm, Purple (1), Mauve (2), Fuchsia (3), Emerald (4), Mid Blue (5), Turquoise (6) 75gm of each. 6 buttons.

NEEDLES One pair of 4½mm (no. 7) needles and one pair of 5½mm (no.5) needles. Stitch holders.

TENSION Using 5½mm (no.5) needles and measured over pattern, 16 sts and 20 rows = 10cm square (4in square).

BACK

Using 4½mm (no. 7) needles and M, cast on 79 sts and work in k1, p1 rib for 10cm (4in), increasing 18 sts evenly across the last row of rib (97 sts).
Change to 5½mm (no. 5) needles and cont in st st in a pattern of navy (M) chevron stripes with a background of 10-row horizontal stripes in various contrasts (indicated by C on the chart). These C stripes change colour every 10 rows and are worked in the following sequence: 5,2,6,1,4,3,2,6,5,1,3 and 4. Work in chevron pattern from chart, placing the chevron as follows. On RS rows, work from P to U, and on WS rows from U to P. The 24 rows of the chart form the pattern for the chevrons. Cont in pattern, changing C every 10 rows, until 120 rows in pattern have been worked from the beg. **Shape shoulders.**
Next row: cast off 30 sts in pattern, k6 in colour 4 including st on needle after cast-off, 12M, 1 col 4, (12M, 12 col 4) twice.
Next row: cast off 30 sts in pattern, p5 col 4 including st on needle after cast-off, 12M, 3 col 4, 12M, 5 col 4. Leave rem 37 sts on a spare needle.

LEFT FRONT

Using 4½mm (no. 7) needles and M, cast on 49 sts. Work 10cm (4in) in single rib as for back, ending with a RS row.
Next row (RS): rib 10, leave these sts on a safety pin, rib 3, *inc in next st, rib 3; rep from * to last 4 sts, inc in next st rib 3 (48 sts).
Change to 5½mm (no. 5) needles and cont in a pattern of diagonal M stripes slanted to right (side edge), with a background of C stripes, which should be worked in the same colour sequence as back. Work in pattern from chart, working RS rows from P to R, and WS rows from R to P. Thus first 2 rows will be:
Row 1 (RS): k(12C,12M) twice.
Row 2: p1C,p12M,p12C,p12M,p11C.
Working the diagonal stripe pattern as the 24 rows of chart and, changing C every 10 rows, cont until 103 rows in pattern have been worked from beg, thus ending with a knit row. **Shape neck.**
Row 104: cast off 5 sts, pattern to end.
Pattern 1 row straight then dec 1 st at neck edge on every row until you have 30 sts. Cont straight until 120 rows in pattern have been worked from beg. Cast off.

RIGHT FRONT

Cast on as for left front and work 3cm (1¼in) in rib as back, ending with a WS row.
Next row (buttonhole): rib 4, k2tog, rib to end.
Cont in rib (casting on 1 st over the one cast off on the previous row) until rib measures 10cm (4in), ending with a RS row.
Next row: rib 3,* inc in next st, rib 3, rep from * to last 14 sts, inc in next st, rib 3, turn, leaving rem 10 sts on a safety pin.
Change to 5½mm (no. 5) needles and cont in pattern of diagonal M stripes slanting to left (side edge) and multicoloured C stripes, reading chart from S to U on RS rows, and from U to S on WS rows. Thus the first 2 rows will be:
Row 1 (RS): k(12M,12C) twice.
Row 2: p11C,12M,12C,12M,1C. Cont in pattern as now set until 104 rows have been worked from beg, finishing with a WS row. **Shape neck.**
105th row: cast off 5 sts, pattern to end.
Dec 1 st at neck edge on every row until you have 30 sts. Cont straight until front matches back to shoulder. Cast off.

SLEEVES

(Both alike.) Using 4½mm (no. 7) needles and M, cast on 37 sts and work 10cm (4in) in rib as for back, inc 16 sts evenly across last row of rib (53 sts).
Change to 5½mm (no. 5) needles and cont in pattern of M chevrons with 10-row C stripes in foll sequence: 1,6,2,3,4,5, reading M for C and C for M, and foll chart from Q to T on RS rows and from T to Q on WS rows. Thus the first 2 rows will be:
Row 1 (RS): k2C, k12M, k12C, k1M, k12C, k12M, k2C.
Row 2: p1C, p12M, p12C, p3M, p12C, p12M, p1C.
Inc at each end of the fifth and every foll fourth row as indicated on chart (63 sts). Keeping pattern correct, inc 1 st each end of next and every foll fourth row to 81 sts. Work 3 rows straight, thus completing 60 rows of pattern. Cast off loosely.

FRONT BANDS

Return to 10 sts on safety pin at end of left front welt, sl them on to a 4½mm (no. 7) needle (point to inner edge). Join M.

Row 1: inc 1, rib to end, cont in rib on these 11 sts until band, when slightly stretched, fits up left front to start of neck shaping.

Leave sts on safety pin and sew band to front. Mark band with pins to indicate buttons, the first 3cm (1¼in) from beg and the last approx 6cm (2½in) from neck shaping (this will be in the neck band) and 4 more spaced equally between. Sl the 10 sts from safety pin at end of right front welt on to a 4½mm (no. 7) needle, point to inner edge. Join M and work first row as left front band.

Cont in rib on these 11 sts, making buttonholes to match pin positions as follows. From outer edge, rib 4, k2tog, rib to end. Cont in rib (casting on 1 st over that cast off on next row) until band reaches neck shaping. Leave sts on safety pin and sew band to front.

NECKBAND

Join shoulder seams, taking care to match stripes. With RS facing and using 4½mm (no. 7) needles and M, rib 11 sts from right front band, pick up and knit 20 sts up right neck edge, knit 37 sts from back neck, pick up and knit 20 sts down left neck edge, rib 11 sts from left front band (99 sts).

Cont in rib until band measures 6cm (2½in), ending at right front edge. On next row make buttonhole as previously. Work another 6cm (2½in), ending at right front edge, then make another buttonhole on next row. Work 6cm (2½in) more in rib, ending with a WS row. Cast off in rib.

MAKING UP

Join sleeves to body, join side and sleeve seams. Turn neckband in half to the WS and slipstitch into place. Neaten double buttonhole.

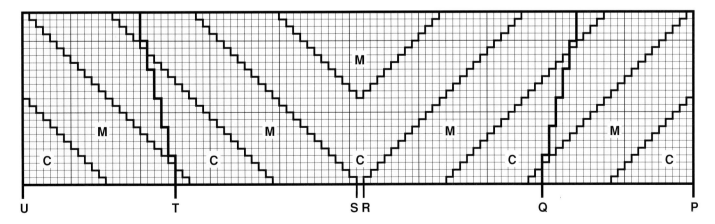

Key M = Navy (main colour)   C = Contrast colour as given in pattern

'SOFTLY SPEAKING' JACKET

Soft as a whisper, this muted spring jacket has simple flower motifs. The curved shape is slimming, and it is worked using the fairisle method (see p. 9), with no chart to follow.

BACK

Using 5½mm (no. 5) needles and A, cast on 109 sts.
Row 1: knit in A.
Row 2: purl in A.
Row 3: k1B, *k11A, k1B, rep from * to end.
Row 4: p2B, *p9A, p3B, rep from * to last 2 sts, p2B.
Row 5: k2B, *k1A, k2B, k3A, k2B, k1A, k3B, rep from * to last 2 sts, k2B.
Row 6: p6B, *p1A, p11B, rep from * to last 6 sts, p6B.
Rows 7 and 8: 4B, *5A, 7B, rep to last 4 sts, 4B.
Rows 9 and 10: 3B, *7A, 5B, rep from * to last 3 sts, 3B.
Row 11: as row 3.
Row 12: p2B,* p2A, p1B, p3A, p1B, p2A, p3B, rep from * to last 2 sts, p2B.
Row 13: k5B,* k3A, k9B, rep from * to last 5 sts, k5B.
Row 14: as row 6.
Rows 15 and 16: work in B.
These 16 rows form the pattern.
Rows 17–32: work in pattern, using C instead of B.
Rows 33–48: work in pattern, using D instead of B.
Rows 49–64: work in pattern, using E instead of B.
Rows 65–80: work in pattern, using F instead of B.
Rows 81–96: work in pattern, using G instead of B; mark each end of row 82 to denote the end of the side seams.
Rows 97–112: work in pattern, using H instead of B.
Rows 113–128: work in pattern, using J instead of B. **Slope shoulders.**

Cont in J only, cast off 18 sts at beg of each of the next 4 rows. Cast off rem 37 sts.

LEFT FRONT

Using 5½mm (no. 5) needles and A, cast on 9 sts.
Row 1: knit in A.
Row 2: using A, cast on 8 sts, purl these sts, purl to end (17 sts).
Row 3: k1B, k11A, k1B, k4A.
Row 4: using A, cast on 6 sts, purl these sts, p3A, p3B, p9A, p2B (23 sts).
Row 5: k2B, k1A, k2B, k3A, k2B, k1A, k3B, k1A, k2B, k3A, k2B, k1A.
Row 6: using B, cast on 6 sts, purl these sts, p4B, p1A, p11B, p1A, p6B (29 sts).
These 6 rows set the position of the pattern for the left front. **
Work pattern as set, with colour sequence to match back, taking extra sts into pattern as they occur.
Row 7: knit in pattern.
Row 8: cast on 4 sts at front edge. Then, keeping pattern as set, cast on 3 sts at front edge on foll alt row and 2 sts on next alt row (38 sts).
Next row: work in pattern (omit this row when working the right front).
Inc 1 st at front edge on each of the next 12 rows and then on 5 foll alt rows (55 sts). Work in pattern for a further 38 rows.**
Shape front edge.
Dec 1 st at beg of next row and the 4 foll alt rows (50 sts). Mark the **end** of the last row to denote end of side seam.
Work in pattern for 1 row, then dec 1 st at front edge of next row and the 13 foll alt rows (36 sts). Work in pattern for a further 18 rows. **Slope shoulder.**
Cont in J only, cast off 18 sts at beg of the next row (18 sts).
Work in pattern for 1 row, cast off rem sts.

RIGHT FRONT

Using 5½mm (no. 5) needles and A, cast on 9 sts.
Row 1: knit in A.
Row 2: purl in A.
Row 3: using A, cast on 8 sts and work these sts as follows: k4A, k1B, k3A, k8A, k1B (17 sts).
Row 4: p2B, p9A, p3B, p3A.
Row 5: using B, cast on 6 sts and work these sts as follows: k1A, k2B, k3A, k2B, k1A, k3B, k1A, k2B, k3A, k2B, k1A, k2B (23 sts).
Row 6: p6B, p1A, p11B, p1A, p4B.
Row 7: using B, cast on 6 sts and work these sts as follows: k1A, k5B, k2B, k5A, k7B, k5A, k4B (29 sts).

These 7 rows set the position of the pattern for the right front. Work from ** to ** (noting exception in brackets). **Shape front edge.**
Dec 1 st at end of next row and the 4 foll alt rows (50 sts). Mark the **beginning** of the last row to denote end of side seam.
Work in pattern for 1 row, then dec 1 st at front edge on next row and the 13 foll alt rows (36 sts). Work in pattern for a further 18 rows. **Slope shoulder.**
Cont in J only, cast off 18 sts at beg of the next row (18 sts). Work in pattern for 1 row, cast off rem sts.

SLEEVES

(Both alike.) Using 5mm (no. 6) needles and A, cast on 48 sts. Knit 4 rows. Work in rib as follows.
Row 1 of rib: *k6, p6, rep from * to end.
Rep row 1 of rib 24 times more.
Next row: rib 3, inc, * rib 2, inc, rep from * until last 2 sts, rib 2 (63 sts).
Change to 5½mm (no. 5) needles and work in pattern as follows.
Row 1: knit in A.
Row 2: purl in A.
Row 3: inc with A, *k1B, k11A, rep from * to last 2 sts, k1B, inc with A (65 sts).
Row 4: p1A, *p3B, p9A, rep from * to last 4 sts, p3B, p1A.
Row 5: k1A, k3B, *k1A, k2B, k3A, k2B, k1A, k3B, rep from * to last st, k1A.
Row 6: inc with B, p7B, *p1A, p11B, rep from * to last 9 sts, p1A, p7B, inc with B (67 sts).
These 6 rows set the position of the pattern for the sleeves. Work pattern as set, with colour sequence to match back, taking extra sts into pattern as they occur. Work 2 rows in pattern. Inc 1 st at each end of the next row and the 13 foll third rows (95 sts). Work in pattern for a further 16 rows. Cast off in E.

BORDER

Join shoulder seams. Using 5mm (no. 6) needles and A, cast on 30 sts. Work in rib as follows.
Row 1: k6, *p6, k6, rep from * to end.
Row 2: p6, *k6, p6, rep from * to end.
Rep the last 2 rows until border, when stretched slightly, reaches across half of centre back neck, down left front around the curved edge of left front, across lower edge (the cast-on edge of the back), around the curved edge of right front and across the rem half of centre back neck. Cast off in rib.

MAKING UP

Sew on border, joining cast-on and cast-off edges tog at centre back neck. Sew cast-off edge of sleeves to row ends between markers on back and left and right fronts. Join sleeve and side seams, matching the pattern.

Inca Jacket

I wanted to design a 'knit it yourself' duffel jacket, based on woven ethnic textiles. I experimented using bright colours and muted alpaca neutrals, and the results were so different that I decided to include photographs of both in this collection. The pattern for this design is also available as a Bond machine-knit pattern and is included in their magazine *Knitting in the '90s*. Bond is the only machine I have come across that can properly handle handknit yarns without completely flattening them, and it is simple to use too.

SIZE To fit up to 102cm (40in) bust. Actual size: 132cm (52in) bust; 69cm (27in) long; 44.5cm (17½in) sleeve seam.

MATERIALS Melinda Coss Mohair: Brown/Black (A) 325gm, Light Grey/Turquoise (B) 155gm, Ecru/Red (C) 95gm, Dark Grey/Gold (D) 50gm. 7 buttons.

NEEDLES One pair of 4½mm (no. 7) needles and one pair of 5½mm (no. 5) needles. Stitch holder.

TENSION Using 5½mm (no. 5) needles and measured over pattern, 15 sts and 17 rows = 10cm square (4in square)

BACK

Using 4½mm (no. 7) needles and A, cast on 98 sts. Work in k2, p2 rib for 6 rows. Change to 5½mm (no. 5) needles and work in st st as follows:
2 rows B, 3 rows C, 2 rows B, 3 rows A, 1 row D, 2 rows C, 5 rows B, 4 rows C. Work 2 more rows in B then, using B as your background throughout, place chart 1 as follows.*
Next row (RS): k5B, k41 sts of chart, k8B, repeat 41 sts of chart, k5B.
Keeping chart in this position, work the 19 rows until it is complete. St st 2 rows in B, change to A, st st 23 rows, cast off all sts.

RIGHT FRONT

Using 4½mm (no. 7) needles and A, cast on 50 sts. Work as for back to *.

Next row: k4B, k41 sts of chart 1, k5B.
Keeping chart in this position, cont foll pattern as for back until 23 rows of A are complete. Cast off all sts.

LEFT FRONT

Work as for right front but place chart 1 as follows: k5B, k41 sts of chart, k4B.

YOKE

(Starting at back.) Using 5½mm (no. 5) needles and A, cast on 100 sts. St st 8 rows in A.

Keeping background colour in A, place chart 2 as follows: k9A, knit across 33 sts of chart 2, k16A, repeat 33 sts of chart 2, k9A. Work 28 rows of chart in this position. St st 8 more rows in A, 3 in B, 2 in D, 3 in C, 2 in D. **Shape neck.**

Next row (RS): k35D, leave remaining sts on a spare needle and, working on this first set of 35 sts only, purl 1 row D. Inc 1 st at the end of the next row and, at the same edge, on the 4 foll third rows.

At the same time work in stripe sequence as follows: 3 rows B, 2 rows C, 3 rows D, cont in B only. When increases are complete you should have 40 sts. St st 3 rows, turn, cast on 10 sts at the end of the next row (neck edge).** Purl 1 row, place chart 2 as follows: k9B, k33 sts of chart 2, k8B. Work the 28 rows of chart in this position, st st 5 rows B, cast off.**

Rejoin yarn to wrong side on remaining sts. Keeping in stripe sequence as for other side of neck, cast off centre 30 sts, purl to end. Cont in st st, inc 1 st at neck edge on next row and 4 foll third rows. Then inc 10 sts at neck edge on foll third row. Work as for other side from ** to **.

Join lower half of fronts to fronts on yoke with a narrow backstitch on the right side, so that you have a narrow ridge. Join back to yoke in the same way.

SLEEVES

(Both alike.) Using 4½mm (no. 7) needles and A, cast on 40 sts. Work in k2, p2 rib for 10cm (4in), increasing 2 sts on last row of rib (42 sts).

Change to 5½mm (no. 5) needles and cont in st st, working in stripe sequence as for back to *. **At the same time**, inc 1 st each end of every alt row 10 times, then every third row until you have 86 sts. When stripe sequence is complete you should have 64 sts.

Next row (RS): k12, knit across 41 sts of chart, k11. Work the 19 rows of chart in this position, then work 2 more rows in B. Change to A. Complete increases, then st st 4 more rows in A. Cast off all sts.

BUTTONBAND

Using 4½mm (no. 7) needles and A, cast on 8 sts. Work in k2, p2 rib until band fits neatly up left front to neck shaping when slightly stretched. Cast off and slipstitch neatly to left front edge. With pins, mark positions for 7 buttons, the first 3 rows down from the top and the last 8 rows up from the bottom, with the other five spaced evenly between.

BUTTONHOLE BAND

Work as for buttonband, making buttonholes as follows to correspond with pins.
Buttonhole row 1: k2, p1, cast off 2, k1, p2.
Row 2: k2, p1, cast on 2, k1, p2.
When band is complete, cast off and slipstitch neatly to right front.

COLLAR

Using 4½mm (no. 7) needles and A and with RS of work facing, begin halfway across top of buttonband and pick up and knit approx 100 sts all around the neck to centre of buttonhole band. Work in k2, p2 rib for 6 rows, change to 5½mm (no. 5) needles and cont in rib until work measures 12cm (4¾in) from start. Cast off in rib.

MAKING UP

Using a narrow backstitch, join sleeves to jacket. Join side and sleeve seams.

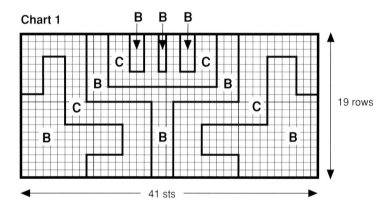

Chart 1

41 sts — 19 rows

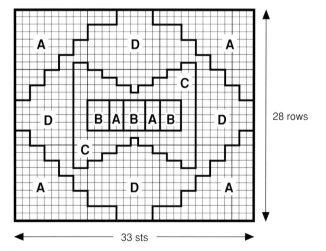

Chart 2

33 sts — 28 rows

Key
A = Brown/Black B = Light Grey/Turquoise
C = Ecru/Red D = Dark Grey/Gold

CLASSIC CREW-NECKED CARDIGAN AND SWEATER

These two classic shapes form the basis for many of my designs. The dropped sleeve is sensible for a cardigan, since it can be worn over a number of garments and is useful for all seasons. You could add your own design ideas to these shapes. How about using up oddments in rainbow stripes or adding some cables?

SIZE To fit bust 86–102cm (34–40in). Actual size: 104cm (41in) bust; 68cm (27in) long; 53cm (21in) sleeve seam.

MATERIALS Melinda Coss Mohair: 450gm (cardigan), 425gm (jumper). 8 buttons.

NEEDLES One pair of 4½mm (no. 7) needles and one pair 6mm (no. 4) needles. Stitch holder.

TENSION Using 6mm (no. 4) needles and measured over st st, 16 sts and 18 rows = 10cm square (4in square).

CARDIGAN

BACK
Using 4½mm (no. 7) needles, cast on 70 sts. Work in k1, p1 rib for 15 rows.
Next row: work in k1, p1 rib, inc in the first st and every foll fifth st (84 sts).
Change to 6mm (no. 4) needles and, starting with a knit row, work in st st* for 104 rows. **Shape shoulder.**
Cast off 13 sts at beg of the next 2 rows and 14 sts at beg of the foll 2 rows. Cast off remaining 30 sts.

RIGHT FRONT
Using 4½mm (no. 7) needles, cast on 36 sts. Work in k1, p1 rib for 15 rows. Rib one more row, inc 6 sts evenly across it (42 sts). Change to 6mm (no. 4) needles and, starting with a knit row, work in st st for 98 rows. **Shape neck.**
Row 99: cast off 7 sts at beg of this row, 2 sts at beg of the next alt row and 1 st at neck edge on the foll 4 rows. Continuing to

dec 1 st at neck edge on the next 2 rows, cast off 13 sts at shoulder edge on next row and 14 sts at shoulder edge on the foll alt row.

LEFT FRONT
Work as for right front but start your neck shaping on row 98.

SLEEVES

(Both alike.) Using 4½mm (no. 7) needles, cast on 36 sts. Work in k1, p1 rib for 15 rows. Rib 1 more row, inc 18 sts evenly across it (54 sts). Change to 6mm (no. 4) needles and, starting with a knit row, work in st st, inc 1 st each end of every fourth row until you have 84 sts. Work straight until sleeve measures 53cm (21in) from cast-on edge. Cast off loosely. Join shoulder seams using a flat seam.

NECKBAND

With RS of work facing and using 4½mm (no. 7) needles, pick up 17 sts from right front neck, 30 sts across back and 17 sts down left front neck (64 sts). Work in k1, p1 rib for 10 rows. Cast off loosely in rib. Turn neckband inwards and slipstitch cast-off edge to pick-up edge.

BUTTONBAND

Using 4½mm (no. 7) needles, cast on 8 sts. Work in k1, p1 rib until band fits to top of neckband when slightly stretched. Cast off in rib.
With pins, mark positions for 8 buttons, the first one 5 rows from the bottom of the band and the last one 3 rows down from the top of the band, with the 6 others spaced evenly in between.

BUTTONHOLE BAND

Using 4½mm (no. 7) needles, cast on 8 sts. Work in k1, p1 rib for 4 rows.
Row 5: rib 3, cast off 2, rib 3.
On return row, rib 3, cast on 2, rib 3. Cont in rib, making buttonholes to correspond with pins on buttonband as described above. When band matches buttonband at neck edge, cast off.

MAKING UP

Join sleeves to body. Join side and sleeve seams using a narrow backstitch. Sew buttonband and buttonhole band into position.

SWEATER

Work back and sleeves as for cardigan.

FRONT

Work as for back to * st st for 96 rows.
Row 97: k31 sts, leave remaining sts on a spare needle and, working on this first set of sts only, dec 1 st at neck edge on next 6 rows. Purl 1 row. Keeping neck edge straight, **shape shoulder.** Cast off 14 sts at beg of next row and 13 sts at beg of the foll alt row. Return to held sts and slip centre 23 sts on to a spare

needle. Rejoin yarn and repeat shaping for other side of neck. Join right shoulder seam.

NECKBAND

With RS of work facing and 4½mm (no. 7) needles, pick up and knit 10 sts down left front neck, 23 sts held for centre front, 10 sts up right front neck and 34 sts across back neck. Work in k1, p1 rib for 10 rows. Cast off loosely.
Join left shoulder seam, turn neckband inwards and slipstitch cast-off edge to pick-up edge.

MAKING UP

Join sleeves to body. Join side and sleeve seams using a narrow backstitch.

JIGSAW JACKET

This boxy jacket has a Sixties flavour and looks super-smart over a black skirt or trousers. As with the Argyll coat (p. 50), it is a new interpretation of a classic design, this time using the traditional dogtooth pattern. It is knitted in a combination of intarsia and fairisle (i.e. you can carry the yarn across the back of small areas, but should use separate balls if the gap is larger than five stitches).

SIZE To fit bust 86–102cm (34–40in). Actual size: 125cm (49in) bust; 56cm (22in) long; 49cm (19¼in) sleeve.

MATERIALS Melinda Coss Mohair: Black (A) 300gm, Emerald 90gm, Royal 75gm, Fuchsia 75gm. 6 round buttons.

NEEDLES One pair of 4½mm (no. 7) needles and one pair of 5½mm (no. 5) needles. Stitch holder.

TENSION Using 5½mm (no. 5) needles and measured over pattern, 16 sts and 21 rows = 10cm square (4in square)

BACK

Using 4½mm (no. 7) needles and A (black), cast on 104 sts.
Work in k1, p1 rib for 3.5cm (1½in).
Change to 5½mm (no. 5) needles and begin foll chart from row 1, using small balls of yarn for each colour. NB Do not carry main yarn across back of coloured areas.

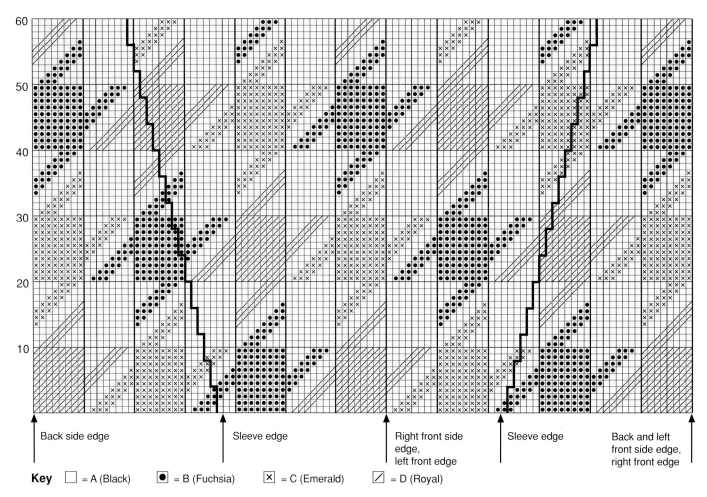

Back side edge — Sleeve edge — Right front side edge, left front edge — Sleeve edge — Back and left front side edge, right front edge

Key □ = A (Black)   ● = B (Fuchsia)   ⊠ = C (Emerald)   ⧄ = D (Royal)

Work rows 1–60 in st st, then repeat from row 1 until back measures 29cm (11½in) from cast-on edge, finishing with a WS row. **Shape armholes.**

Keeping in pattern, dec 1 st at each end of the next 8 rows (88 sts). Cont straight until armhole measures 27cm (10½in), ending with a WS row. Cast off 30 sts, cut off yarn and slip next 28 sts on to a holder, join in yarn to next st, cast off remaining 30 sts.

LEFT FRONT

Using 4½mm (no. 7) needles and A, cast on 48 sts. Work in k1, p1 rib for 3.5cm (1½in). Change to 5½mm (no. 5) needles and work from chart as before, noting instructions for left front. Cont until front measures same as back to armhole, ending with a WS row. **Shape armhole.**

Keeping pattern correct, dec 1 st at beg of the next row and at same edge on foll 7 rows (40 sts). Cont straight until front edge measures 50cm (19½in) from cast-on edge, ending with a RS row. **Shape neck.**

Keeping pattern correct, cast off 4 sts at beg of next row and 2 sts at beg of the foll 3 alt rows (30 sts). Cont straight until front measures same as back to shoulder, ending with a WS row. Cast off.

RIGHT FRONT

Work as for left front, reversing all shapings.

SLEEVES

(Both alike.) Using 4½mm (no. 7) needles and A, cast on 44 sts. Work in k1, p1 rib for 3.5cm (1½in).

Change to 5½mm (no. 5) needles and work from chart, foll instructions for sleeves. **At the same time** inc 1 st at each end of next and every foll fourth row until you have 86 sts.

Cont straight until sleeve measures 45.5cm (17¾in) from cast-on edge, ending with a WS row. Keeping pattern correct, dec 1 st at each end of the next 8 rows (70 sts). Cast off.

NECKBAND

With RS facing and using 4½mm (no. 7) needles and A, pick up and knit 16 sts from right front neck, knit across back neck stitches on holder, pick up and knit 16 sts from left front neck (60 sts). Work in k1, p1 rib for 3.5cm (1½in). Cast off in rib.

BUTTONBAND

Using 4½mm (no. 7) needles and A, cast on 9 sts. Work in k1, p1 rib until band, when slightly stretched, fits along left front.

Cast off in rib.

Mark 6 button positions, the first 3cm (1¼in) from lower edge, the last 2cm (¾in) from cast-off (neck) edge, and the remaining 4 spaced evenly in between.

BUTTONHOLE BAND

Work as for buttonband, working buttonholes to correspond with markers as follows.

Buttonhole row 1 (RS): rib 4, cast off 2, rib to end.

Buttonhole row 2: rib, casting on 2 sts over those cast off in previous row.

MAKING UP

Using narrow backstitch, join sleeves to jacket, join sleeve and side seams. Sew front bands into position. Sew on buttons.

RING-A-ROUND COAT

This three-quarter-length coat has a cosy turned-down collar and a one-button loop fastener. It is worked using the intarsia method (see p. 8). The full shape makes it the perfect cover-up for chilly autumn evenings.

SIZE To fit bust 86–107cm (34–42in). Actual size: 130cm (51in) bust; 88cm (35in) long; 37cm (14½in) sleeve with cuff turned back.

MATERIALS Melinda Coss Mohair: Black (A) 450gm, Turquoise (B) 50gm, Royal (C) 50gm, Mid Blue (D) 60gm, Purple (E) 100gm, Mauve (F) 100gm, Fuchsia (G) 35gm. 1 large button.

NEEDLES One pair of 4½mm (no. 7) needles, one pair of 5mm (no. 6) needles and one pair of 5½mm (no. 5) needles.

TENSION Using 5½mm (no. 5) needles and measured over pattern, 16 sts and 20 rows = 10cm square (4in square).

BACK

Using 5mm (no. 6) needles and A, cast on 104 sts. *Beg with a knit row, work 7 rows in st st. Knit 1 row to mark hemline. Change to 5½mm (no. 5) needles and, beg with a knit row and

Chart 1

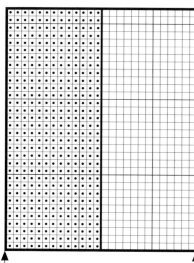

26 sts

Chart 2

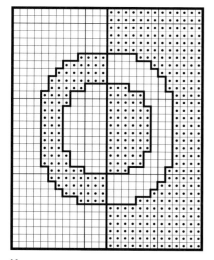

Key

⬛ = A

⬜ = B, C, D, E, F or G as stated in pattern

working in st st throughout, work in pattern bands as follows.
Band 1
Row 1: using A and B (work row 1 of chart 1, then row 1 of chart 2) twice.
Row 2: using A and B (work row 2 of chart 2, then row 2 of chart 1) twice.
Cont in pattern as set until the 32 rows of both charts have been worked.
Band 2
Row 1: using A and C (work row 1 of chart 2, then row 1 of chart 1) twice.
Row 2: using A and C (work row 2 of chart 1, then row 2 of chart 2) twice.
Cont in pattern as set until the 32 rows of both charts have been worked.
Band 3
Work as band 1, using D instead of B.
Band 4
Work as band 2, using E instead of C.
Band 5
Work as band 1, using F instead of B.*
Band 6
Work rows 1–16 of band

2, using G instead of C. **Shape shoulders.**
Keeping band 6 correct, cast off 36 sts at beg of next 2 rows. Leave rem 32 sts on a holder.

LEFT FRONT

Using 5mm (no. 6) needles and A, cast on 52 sts. Working each chart once (instead of twice), work as back from * to *. Work row 1 of band 6. **Shape neck.**
Keeping band 6 correct, cast off 8 sts at beg of next row and 2 sts at beg of foll alt row. Dec 1st at neck edge on next 6 rows (36 sts). Cast off.

RIGHT FRONT

Work as left front but beg neck shaping on row 3 of band 6.

SLEEVES

(Both alike.) Using 4½mm (no. 7) needles and A, cast on 69 sts. Next row: p1, (k1, p1) to end. Rep this row for 10cm (4in), dec 1 st in centre of last row (68 sts).
Change to 5½mm (no. 5) needles and, beg with a knit row, work in st st and pattern bands as follows.
Band 1
Row 1: using A and E, work sts 19–26 from row 1 of chart 2, then work row 1 of chart 1, row 1 of chart 2 and sts 1–8 of chart 1. This row sets the position of the pattern for band 1.
Band 2
Row 1: using A and F, work sts 13–26 from row 1 of chart 1, then work row 1 of chart 2, row 1 of chart 1 and sts 1–14 of chart 2.
Cont in pattern, inc 1 st each end of second and every foll fifth row (82 sts).
Work 4 rows straight. Cast off.

MAKING UP

Join both shoulder seams.
Front facings (make 2): using 5mm (no. 6) needles, A and with RS facing, pick up and knit 146 sts between neck edge and hemline. Beg with a purl row, work 5 rows in st st. Cast off. Fold facing to WS and slipstitch in position.
Collar: using 4½mm (no. 7) needles and A and with RS facing, pick up and knit 63 sts around neck edge, dec 3 sts at back neck. Work 14cm (5½in) in p1, k1 rib as for sleeves. Cast off loosely in rib.
Pockets (make 4): place markers on side seams 29cm (11½in) up from hemline edge on both fronts and back and another set of markers 17cm (6¾in) above them. Using 5mm (no. 6) needles, A and with RS facing, pick up and knit 26 sts between the markers. Beg with a purl row, work 10cm (4in) in st st. Dec 1 st each end of next and every alt row until there are 16 sts. Cast off.
Sew on sleeves, placing centre of sleeves to shoulder seams. Join side seams, taking seams around edges of pockets, then join sleeve seams, reversing seam at cuff for turn-back. Turn up hem at hemline and slipstitch into position. Sew on button at neck edge, making a loop to correspond.

Stockist Information

All the designs in this book are available in kit form by mail order. Kits contain the correct quantities of yarn (you do not need to buy a 50gm ball when only 10gm are needed), designer labels and buttons when appropriate. Since all our kits are packed on receipt of order, you can choose your own colourways from our printed chart. You can also order extra balls of yarn if you wish to lengthen a garment, and mohair also comes on 450gm cones.

For those of you wishing to substitute yarns, be sure to check with your wool shop that the tension on the pattern matches the tension specified by the manufacturer of the yarn you intend buying. This should not prove a problem, since tension does not alter considerably from one brand of mohair to another. Our mohair is a mix of 83 per cent mohair, 9 per cent wool and 8 per cent nylon. Always be sure to buy the best quality that you can afford – your work deserves it.

For those who simply cannot or do not have time to knit up the garments, we offer a ready-made service. Details are available on application. We also offer courses, both residential and day, for knitters who need practical help in mastering the skills. These courses also teach you how to design your own jumpers, and they take place at our studio in the mountains in West Wales.

For full details on all the above write to: Melinda Coss Knitting, Ty'r Waun Bach, Gwernogle, Dyfed, West Wales, SA32 7RY. Tel: 0267 202 386.

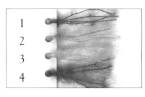

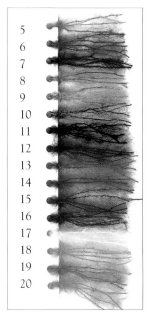

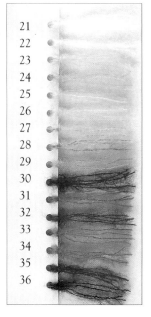

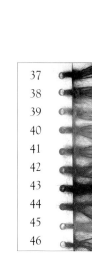

Key

1	Mid Blue	35	Fuchsia
2	Light Blue	36	Bottle Green
3	Lilac	37	Smoke
4	Candy Floss	38	Olive
5	Mauve	39	Apple
6	Purple	40	Lime
7	Navy	41	Dull Jade
8	Slate	42	Blue Smoke
9	Mink	43	Crimson
10	Charcoal	44	Pinky Red
11	Black	45	Coral Rose
12	Chocolate	46	Red
13	Coffee		
14	Rust		
15	Chestnut		
16	Maroon		
17	Oatmeal		
18	Old Gold		
19	Gingy		
20	Orange		
21	Natural		
22	White		
23	Pink		
24	Peach		
25	Lemon		
26	Mint		
27	Azure		
28	Hyacinth		
29	Yellow		
30	Scarlet		
31	Turquoise		
32	Royal		
33	Emerald		
34	Jade		